HORSE CAMP

TIMBER RIDGE RIDERS
Book 11

HORSE CAMP

Maggie Dana

PAGEWORKS PRESS

Horse Camp © 2015 Maggie Dana
www.maggiedana.com

This is a work of fiction. While references may be made to actual
places or events, all names, characters, incidents, and locations
are from the author's imagination and do not resemble any actual
living or dead persons, businesses, or events.
Any similarity is coincidental.

ISBN 978-0-9909498-2-4

Edited by Judith Cardanha
Cover design by Margaret Sunter
Interior designs by Anne Honeywood
Published by Pageworks Press
Text set in Sabon

for Jade

1

A BLUE-AND-GOLD TRAILER delivered the pony at noon. Without missing a beat, the barn's new arrival backed down the ramp and looked around calmly as if she were at home. Her halter's nameplate said "Summer Solstice."

"Sweet," said Holly Chapman. "She's a Norwegian Fjord."

"Looks like it," said Kate McGregor.

That bi-colored mane was a dead giveaway. So were the dorsal stripe along the pony's creamy dun back and the brownish bits at the tips of her cute little ears.

Did she have a barn name?

Summer Solstice was quite a mouthful. Gently, Kate rubbed the pony's nose. Her adorable face was dished, like an Arabian. Standing perfectly still, Summer Solstice gave a contented sigh, and Kate fell in love with her. She was a sucker for cute ponies, especially when they had nice manners.

Behind them, someone laughed. "That's not a horse. It's a dump truck."

Slowly, Kate turned. Trust Angela Dean to be snotty about a horse that wasn't a Danish Warmblood with perfect dressage scores and a pedigree from *Who's Who in the Horse World*.

"For your information," Kate said, "the Norwegian Fjord goes back thousands of years, and—"

"Oh, who cares?" Angela snapped. "It's just another dumb pony." Tossing back a wave of black hair, she linked arms with her best friend, Kristina James, and they sauntered off, giggling the way they always did.

Kate yawned—not because she was tired of Angela and her sarcastic comments, but because she'd flown home to Vermont the day before and her brain hadn't caught up yet. Already, her month in England seemed unreal, like a disjointed dream. Training with her Olympic favorites was the dreamy part; rescuing two kidnapped friends in a thunderstorm had been an absolute nightmare.

"Jet lag," Holly said, yawning as well.

Kate rubbed her eyes. "I want to sleep for a week."

"Me too," Holly said as they led Summer Solstice into the barn. The trailer that had brought her had already left and there was no sign of the pony's owner.

"But we can't. My mother's marrying your dad on Saturday, remember?"

It had all happened so fast that it made Kate's head spin. One minute she and Holly were riding at Beaumont Park; the next, they were flying home a week earlier than planned for a wedding they'd both dreamed of . . . and plotted for.

Kate hadn't even had a chance to ride Buccaneer again. She really missed him. But now, hugging her own horse, Tapestry, and assuring her that she was still number one in Kate's life helped to make up for it. Tapestry whickered.

I. Am. Number. One.

Laughing, Kate fed her chestnut mare a carrot, then ran her hands through Tapestry's flaxen mane and watched Holly settle the new pony—no, horse—into an empty stall across the aisle. Norwegian Fjords were usually pony-sized, but they were classed as horses. This one looked about fourteen hands.

So who owned Summer Solstice?

Had a family with a horse-crazy kid just moved into Timber Ridge? Or was Summer Solstice a new lesson pony for the riding school? They already had three—Plug, Snowball, and Daisy—but could always use another, especially during summer vacation.

Holly's mom, Liz who ran the barn, had told them to expect the Fjord sometime that day. Then, without sharing any more details she'd driven off in her truck to buy grain and to have a last-minute fitting for her wedding gown, leaving both girls brimming with unanswered questions.

Kate tried to picture Liz in a dress. Not easy.

Most of the time, Holly's mom wore boots and old breeches the way Kate did. The only one with any fashion sense was Holly. She looked good in almost anything, including today's ripped jeans and a faded pink t-shirt that said *Boss Mare* on the front.

Kate glanced at her best friend.

In three more days they would be sisters. Before meeting Holly a year ago, Kate had never had a best friend, never mind a sister. She was an only child, with no mother and an absent-minded father who'd always preferred butterflies to people—until he met Liz.

"We'd better hustle," Holly said as she removed the brown shipping bandages from Summer Solstice's sturdy legs.

"Why?" Kate said.

"Because Aunt Bea's waiting."

Kate stifled a groan. She'd forgotten about their date with Aunt Bea's scissors, her pins and tape measure. Holly had sketched ideas for their bridesmaid's dresses on the flight home, then given them to her aunt last night before they'd fallen into bed, totally exhausted. That morning, Kate had woken to the sound of Aunt Bea's sewing machine whirring away in the guest room.

* * *

"Hold still," mumbled Aunt Bea around a mouthful of pins, "or I'll stick you."

Sucking in her breath, Kate tried not to wince. Pins scraped at her sides as she wriggled into layers of soft pink fabric. It felt really odd, like she was climbing into someone else's skin. Through slitted eyes, she glanced at the mirror.

Pink.

It was Holly's favorite color. Kate didn't have a favorite, unless you counted beige, brown, and gray. Barn colors. Oh, and dark green, too, but only because it was part of the Timber Ridge riding team's logo.

"Awesome," Holly said.

Cautiously, Kate looked again. The way Holly had sketched on the plane, discarding one elaborate design after another, Kate had managed to convince herself she'd be wearing a neon pink birthday cake with frosting and sprinkles—and probably candles, as well.

But this wasn't bad.

According to Holly, pink was the best color for both of them. She said it complemented Kate's brown hair and green eyes, and it also looked good with Holly's blue eyes and streaky blond hair. Kate didn't argue. Holly was the expert at this sort of stuff.

Kate glanced at her feet.

Striped socks were fine with paddock boots and breeches, but they didn't look too hot beneath a frou-frou pink dress. Well, not exactly frou-frou. More like—

Helpfully, Holly said, "Totally glam?"

"Yeah," Kate said. "I guess."

And it really was. Her bridesmaid's dress had spaghetti straps, a gathered bodice with a cummerbund, and a softly pleated skirt that swirled around Kate's not very clean knees. It could've been a lot worse—sequins or clouds of itchy chiffon, like the dress Kate had worn at the *Moonlight* premiere.

"You're amazing," Holly said to Aunt Bea, then tried on her own dress, exactly the same as Kate's. Pins stuck out; threads dangled. The hemline dipped in front, so Aunt Bea wielded her scissors.

Snip, snip, snip.

Liz knocked on the door. "Did the Fjord arrive okay?"

"Yes," Holly called out. "But you can't come in."

"Why?"

"Because we're not gonna let you see our dresses until you tell us where you're going on your honeymoon," Holly said. "So *there*." She stuck out her tongue. The door handle rattled, but Holly had already locked it.

"But I don't *know*," came Liz's voice. It held a hint of laughter. "Ben wants it to be a surprise."

Kate bit back a smile.

She knew where they were going. Yesterday, her father had let slip a few things when he drove them home from the airport in Boston. Holly had been in the back seat, texting furiously with her boyfriend, Adam.

"I've been invited to give a lecture about the breeding habits of lunar moths," Dad said, swerving to avoid an oncoming truck. Kate tightened her seatbelt. Her father's driving had always alarmed her.

"Where?" she said.

News like this used to mean long separations, but now that Dad had given up his job at the university and bought a local butterfly museum, he didn't travel any more. Kate liked it better this way. No more disappearing acts into the Amazon for months on end to research rare butterflies while leaving Kate with Dad's sister. Kate loved her Aunt Marion, but—

"Vienna," he said.

"Cool," Kate said. "You can visit the Spanish Riding School, and—"

"I'm not going to Spain. I'll be in Austria."

"That's where the Spanish Riding School is," Kate explained. "*The Miracle of the White Stallions*, remember?"

Dad had rented the movie years ago, not long after her mom died. As far as Kate could remember, he'd slept through most of it.

"That's a good idea. I bet Liz would love—" Dad clapped a hand to his mouth.

"What's wrong?"

"Don't you dare tell her where we're going," he said. "It's a surprise for our honeymoon. And don't tell Holly, either. Promise?"

"Okay, sure," Kate said, closing her eyes. Visions of fairytale castles, snow-capped mountains, and dancing white horses swam into view.

Austria?

It sounded—Kate gulped—so *romantic*.

Never in a million years had she expected this from her father. Kate turned around to make sure that Holly hadn't overheard their conversation, but she was now plugged into her iPod and snapping her fingers.

It was kind of nice, having a secret with Dad.

* * *

As Kate had predicted, Holly tackled her mother the moment she got home. Liz had a garment bag draped over one arm, and she carried a box that was just about the right size for a pair of dressy shoes.

"Let me see." Holly grabbed the box.

Liz snatched it back. "No way."

"Why not?"

"Because—"

Kate burst out laughing. They were like two kids in a sandbox, squabbling over trucks and plastic shovels. She left them arguing in the kitchen and took Liz's garment bag into the living room and laid it carefully across the back of the couch, now piled high with her father's stuff. Kate had already moved in with Holly; Dad would move in after he and Liz got back from their honeymoon.

It would be a tight squeeze, all four of them crammed into Liz's house. It was a tiny, three-bedroom ranch, and it came with her job as the Timber Ridge barn manager. Dad and Liz wanted to make it bigger.

But first, they had to buy it.

Except Kate was convinced that Angela's interfering mother would find a way to block the sale. Mrs. Dean ran the Homeowners' Association and pretty much everything else at Timber Ridge, including the golf course, the tennis courts, and the stables, never mind that she didn't know one end of a horse from the other. The only thing Kate wasn't sure about was the ski area, but Mrs. Dean probably ran that, too.

Voices erupted. "But, Mom, that's crazy."

"What is?" Kate said, racing back into the kitchen.

Suddenly hungry, she grabbed the piece of cold toast she'd abandoned earlier that morning and took a bite. Her internal clock was still upside down, and she couldn't tell if it was time for dinner or breakfast.

Holly opened her mouth, but Liz cut her off. "Mrs. Dean will be running a horse camp while I'm away," she said.

Kate spat crumbs all over the table. "*Horse camp?*" she choked out. "At Timber Ridge?"

"See," Holly said, sounding triumphant. "Kate thinks it's a dumb idea, too."

Kate wasn't too sure what to think.

Her brain was still fuzzy with jetlag, and she was sure
that Holly's was, too. Liz's brain was probably fuzzy as
well, given she had a wedding to get ready for. It had all
happened much faster than expected, thanks to Dad's lecture tour that was now doubling as a honeymoon.

And it made sense.

They'd never have been able to afford a trip to Europe
if the University of Vienna wasn't footing the bill. Kate
crossed her fingers that Liz's passport was up to date. It
would be pretty awful if they got to the airport and
weren't allowed to get on the plane.

Aunt Bea trundled into the kitchen, a yellow tape
measure hanging around her neck. "I heard shouting," she
said. "Is everything all right?"

"Yes," Liz said.

"No," Holly snapped.

"Then I guess you told them what's going on." Aunt
Bea poured a mug of coffee and handed it to Liz. "Looks
like you could use this."

"Thanks." Liz sank into a chair.

Two cell phones pinged at once. Kate checked hers. A
text from Brad Piretti, just about the coolest guy in Winfield.

Where are you?

In all the rush, she'd forgotten to let Brad know she
was coming home early from England. She was about to

text him back when Holly reached for her mother's phone, vibrating on the counter like a windup toy gone mad.

"It's Mrs. Dean," Holly said.

Liz sighed. "I'd better take it."

"No," Holly said, pocketing the phone. "She can wait."

2

"CAN YOU *BELIEVE* IT?" Holly said when they were back in the barn, getting ready to ride. She couldn't wait to hit the hunt course and take the horses swimming at Crescent Lake. It would help take her mind off Mrs. Dean's latest scheme.

From the next stall, Kate said, "She's crazy."

"Yeah," Holly muttered, "like a loon."

Rumors had been bouncing around the barn like ping-pong balls. Robin Shapiro figured they'd have to act as counselors and teach the kids to knit fly bonnets. Gloomily, Sue Piretti said they'd have to share their horses with campers who didn't have their own.

"No way," Holly said. "Nobody rides Magician but me and Kate."

"Why is Mrs. Dean doing this?" Kate had asked before they escaped to the barn.

"To attract more buyers to Timber Ridge," Mom had said.

"With a *horse* camp?"

It didn't make any sense. It wasn't as if a bunch of adults would be sleeping in tents and singing songs around a campfire in some sort of corporate bonding experience. It would be kids, like ten and eleven years old. They didn't buy houses; their parents did.

Maybe that was the point.

Well, whatever it was, Holly's frazzled brain was having a hard time absorbing it all. Vaguely, she'd heard Aunt Bea say that Mrs. Dean had already hired a temporary trainer to take over while Mom was away. She would be arriving on Friday.

"Just in time for the wedding," Holly had said.

Her mother had sighed. "Guess I'd better invite her."

"Mom, we don't even *know* her."

But it turned out they did—kind of. Last summer, Jocelyn Fraser had worked at Larchwood, where Adam rode. According to him, Jocelyn was a total ditz. The barn kids called her *Miss Picture Perfect* because she spent far more time preening in front of a mirror than she did teaching.

Great.

Just what they needed—along with two weeks of spoiled brats and their unruly ponies. Well, except for Summer Solstice. She was a sweetheart. Mom said her owner would be arriving on Sunday with the rest of the campers. They wouldn't be sleeping in tents, either. Mrs. Dean had arranged for the kids to stay with families at Timber Ridge.

"Sounds more like a spa than a camp," Holly muttered to herself as she led Magician outside. "They'll get breakfast in bed while we're mucking stalls and feeding their horses."

Kate was already on Tapestry. "Let's ride through Timber Ridge first."

"Why?" Holly climbed onto Magician. It felt absolutely wonderful to be back on her own horse again. She'd missed him something fierce while she was at Beaumont Park.

"Because I want to see all the changes Liz told us about."

"Okay, sure."

It probably wouldn't amount to much—fresh paint on the club house's front door and a few more bushes, and perhaps the Timber Ridge maintenance crew had finally gotten around to rebuilding the upper barn that had burned down last year. Despite the heat, Holly shivered. They'd almost lost Buccaneer in that fire.

"Yikes," Kate said as they rounded the first bend.

Holly rubbed her eyes and blinked. Everything was familiar, yet different—more like a movie set than real life. Sidewalks sparkled, roads gleamed, and all the houses had lawns that were greener than lawns needed to be. Not a stray leaf or a blade of grass out of place.

Topiary bushes shaped like circus animals pranced along the edge of Angela Dean's driveway. Next door, at the James's house, a waterfall trickled over pink rocks and splashed into pools filled with lilies the size of feed buckets. Magician shied at a brick-covered mailbox. What happened to the old metal blue one that Holly used to post letters in on her way to the bus stop?

"Holy ravioli," she said.

The houses at Timber Ridge had always been pretty fancy—far nicer than her own house—but this was insane. Even the faux gas lamps were brand spanking new and festooned with baskets of flowers—real ones, not plastic. For a few disorienting minutes Holly felt as if she'd just landed in Oz. All it needed was a yellow-brick road, a tin man, and a couple of munchkins.

As if on cue, two little boys in matching red t-shirts rode by on green tricycles, followed closely by a woman in a blue dress and sensible shoes, pushing an English pram like the ones that Holly had seen in London.

Was she a nanny? Mary Poppins?

Holly didn't recognize her or the kids. That was odd.

She'd lived at Timber Ridge all her life and knew pretty much everyone. Maybe this family had just moved in. Both horses pricked their ears and snorted as the elegant black pram glided silently past.

"Horses are scared of only two things," Kate said as she patted Tapestry's neck. "Things that move and things that don't."

This joke had been around the barn forever, yet it still made Holly laugh. But inside she was worried. Was Mrs. Dean trying to turn Timber Ridge into a billionaire's horsey playground like the one down in North Carolina with polo fields, fox hunting, and big-name trainers that she'd read about in *Chronicle of the Horse*? If so, Mom was doomed.

She couldn't compete with that.

* * *

As they rode toward the mountain, Kate looked up. Timber Ridge wasn't the highest peak in Vermont, but it had some of the steepest trails, with names like *Devil's Leap*, *Jaws of Death*, and *Plummet*. Last winter had been Kate's first time on skis. She'd taken a wrong turn and gone down a black-diamond run by mistake.

Brad Piretti—whose parents ran the ski area—had found her stranded behind a mogul on *Nightmare* with a bashed-up knee. It had almost wrecked her chances at qualifying for the Festival of Horses—and from skiing again. But she'd swallowed her fear and given it another try on St. Patrick's Day—and that's when Brad kissed her, amid visions of shamrocks and rainbows and snow-capped trees.

He'd kissed her again, a month ago.

It was the night before she flew to England with Holly, and Brad had driven her home from the barn in his truck. But a couple of Brad's classmates had ruined the moment by whistling and giving him a thumbs-up as if Kate were some sort of prize.

She hated that.

This boy–girl thing was so complicated. Horses were a whole lot easier. They didn't complain if you forgot their carrots or paid more attention to a pony across the aisle. They were always just *there*, waiting patiently for you to love them all over again.

Tapestry whinnied at Magician. They were best friends. They shared adjacent stalls in the barn, nibbled on one another's manes, and spent hours in the back paddock standing nose to tail and swishing flies off each other. Magician refused to load onto the trailer unless Tapestry was already on board, which was no big deal given they always went to the same shows and events.

Behind them, two more horses trotted up and Kate turned to find Sue on Tara, her Appaloosa mare, and Robin with Chantilly. Looking glum, Sue nodded toward Angela's three-story mansion with its prancing shrubbery, immaculate lawn, and stone lions guarding the front door.

"So, what do you think?"

"Tacky," Holly said. "Worse than Disneyland."

Kate glanced at her, kind of surprised. Holly loved glitz and glamour, and Kate figured she'd be all over Timber Ridge's flashy new look. Kate couldn't care less. It didn't matter to her what sort of house she lived in as long as they were all together and it was within walking distance of the barn.

Robin pulled a face. "Mrs. Dean told my mother to take down our clothesline."

"Why?" Kate said.

In a whiny voice that mimicked Mrs. Dean's, Robin said, "It degrades our lovely neighborhood to have residents' intimate garments hanging outside for everyone to see."

Kate giggled and Holly laughed so hard she almost fell off her horse. But Sue just sat there. No reaction, nothing. She yanked at Tara's reins, then whirled around and trotted off.

"What's up with her?" Holly said.

"Dunno." Robin patted Chantilly's gray neck. "She's been in a bad mood ever since we flubbed our dressage tests at the Hampshire Classic."

"Was Liz mad at her?"

"No, but Mrs. Dean was," Robin said. "She had a

total meltdown, and then she yelled at Angela for messing up in the jumping."

"That's a first," Holly said.

Kate wondered if this was what had triggered Mrs. Dean's latest scheme. But that was crazy. Just because your riding team lost a challenge cup didn't mean you had to give the entire neighborhood a facelift and invite spoiled little rich kids to a horse camp.

Would Angela be a counselor?

Somehow, Kate couldn't imagine the barn's princess helping the younger girls. Angela had been totally rotten to Marcia, her eleven-year-old stepsister who now lived in New York with her father. Was she coming to the horse camp as well? Kate hoped so. She liked Marcia, and so did Tapestry.

* * *

It was so hot that they decided to bypass the hunt course and head straight for Crescent Lake. On its tiny beach, they stripped down to their bathing suits, took off the horses' saddles, and swapped their bridles for the old nylon halters they'd brought along.

Sue and Tara were first into the water, followed by Holly and Magician, who promptly splashed like a toddler before lying down. He'd done the same with Kate when she'd ridden him in her screen test for the stunt-double role in *Moonlight* last summer. And whenever you rode him through water on a cross-country course, you had to keep him going or you'd end up taking an unexpected dip.

Once they were all thoroughly soaked, Kate and Holly told the other girls about their adventures in England.

"You met a real live princess?" Robin said, shaking water from her mop of brown curls. "What's her name?"

"Isabel DuBois," Holly said. "But we called her Twiggy."

Ignoring Sue's stony expression, Kate explained how Twiggy and Adam had been kidnapped and then abandoned on Smuggler's Island. "It had lots of caves, and Holly figured that's where they were, so we swam the horses out to rescue them."

"In a wicked storm," Holly added.

Kate went on, "And then we lost Spud."

"Who?"

"Holly's horse," Kate said. "He was black, just like Magician, but Jen found him on another beach, chatting up a bunch of tourists."

Jennifer West, another riding team member, was still in England and wouldn't be home until school began in September. She'd asked Kate to exercise her chestnut gelding, Rebel. He was the barn's favorite horse because he loved to eat vanilla pudding, and the little kids spoiled him rotten.

"Sounds like a blast," Robin said. Sue merely shrugged.

"And totally scary," Holly said. "The guys who kidnapped Adam and Twiggy were *pirates*."

"Were *not*," Kate said. "Adam called them *The Three Stooges*, remember?"

But Holly was right. It *had* been scary, never mind that the kidnappers had abducted the wrong kids. It happened when Holly, Adam, and Twiggy were at the *Moonlight* premiere in London with Kate's old movie star boyfriend, Nathan Crane. He and Adam were best friends; they also looked amazingly alike. So did Twiggy and Nathan's costar, Tess O'Donnell.

So they'd pulled a switch.

Wearing Tess's glamorous white ball gown, Twiggy had left the hotel on Adam's arm to a battery of fans and photographers. The limo had whisked them away but hadn't brought them back as planned. It had taken the kidnappers three days to realize they'd snatched the wrong kids, and then they'd dumped them on Smuggler's Island, tied up in a cave that would flood at high tide.

"Wow," Robin said. "Double wow."

Sue pinned Kate with a look. "Does this mean you're back with Nathan Crane?"

"No," Kate said. "He's dating the princess."

"They're like *Beauty and the Beast*," Holly said. "She's totally besotted with him."

But Sue didn't look convinced. She squabbled with her big brother all the time, but when it came to Brad's love life, she was super protective. If a girl even thought about dumping him, all of Sue's claws came out.

"We're cool," Kate said.

"Who?" Sue's voice held a hint of sarcasm. "You and Nathan Crane?"

"No, silly. Me and Brad."

At least, she hoped they were. He still hadn't gotten back to her about the wedding. Brad was supposed to be an usher, along with Adam Randolph. They'd be wearing gray suits and pink ties that matched the bridesmaids' dresses.

Maybe Brad hated pink.

Sue's brother was the high school's best quarterback and a total rock star on the Timber Ridge half pipe. He wore green-and-yellow football shirts and plaid snowboarding pants, but Kate had never seen him in pink. She was still pondering this when Tapestry's knees buckled and down she went, into the water.

Kate threw herself free.

Sputtering and laughing, she surfaced. This was so much fun—being with her horse and all her friends at the lake.

If only Buccaneer were here as well.

He'd spent two short months at Timber Ridge last summer, and then Kate had run into him again at a horse show in England being abused by his rider. With Holly's help, she'd managed to rescue Buccaneer and get him down to safety at Beaumont Park, where the head trainer said that Kate could go far with this horse.

Like to the Olympics?

That was Kate's dream. But was Tapestry good enough to get her there, or did she need another horse?

Kate pulled herself together.

She was a reasonably talented rider who scored blue ribbons at local shows. Dreaming about the Olympics was off-the-wall crazy. Besides, she would never sell Tapestry, and she couldn't afford to keep two horses.

Problem solved.

The Olympics would have to get along without her.

* * *

When they got back to the barn, Angela and Kristina were in the aisle sitting on a tack trunk, heads bent over Angela's iPad. They didn't notice Kate until she was standing right over them.

"Anything good?" she said.

With an exasperated sigh, Angela snapped the cover shut, but not before Kate caught a peek. They'd been live-streaming a horse show, probably the Fairfield County Classic going on right now in Connecticut. It was a huge event and attracted the best riders from all over the country. Before moving to Vermont, Kate had groomed for girls at her old barn who competed in this show.

"Who's jumping?" she said.

"Lucas Callahan," Kristina blurted. "He's—"

Angela kicked her. "Shut up."

"What's the matter?" Holly said, leading Magician into his stall. "Got a crush on him?"

"None of your business."

"Okay," Kate said. "Just asking."

But after Angela and Kristina ran off, Holly said, "I don't blame her."

"What about?" Kate swapped her mare's bridle for a halter and began to rub her down. Tapestry gave a contented sigh and curled her upper lip when Kate found her favorite tickly spots.

"Crushing on Luke Callahan," Holly said. "He's wicked cute. Don't you know who he is?"

"Of course, I do," Kate said. "He's an awesome rider and his dad's a BNT."

"What's that?"

"Big Name Trainer," Kate said, pleased to think she knew something that Holly didn't. Lucas's father, Sam Callahan, wrote a column for *Chronicle of the Horse*, and Kate hung on his every word. In the past ten years he'd produced three Olympic show jumpers and had a slew of up-and-coming hopefuls, including his sixteen-year-old son.

Last year, Lucas Callahan had captured equestrian headlines by beating riders twice his age at a big show in

Ireland. Before that, he'd aced the junior jumper circuit from Maine to Florida.

Lucas Callahan was already living Kate's dream.

3

ON SATURDAY MORNING, Kate was still fast asleep when Holly slipped out of bed and went into her mother's room to help her get ready. Mom was hopeless with makeup—just like Kate.

"Don't blink," Holly said.

So, of course, Mom blinked. Holly wiped splatters of brown mascara off her mother's cheeks and tried again. She'd already managed to get a touch of mauve shadow onto Mom's lids, and it looked fabulous with her deep blue eyes.

Next came Mom's hair. It was short and naturally blond, and Mom's hairdresser had done a great job with the highlights that Holly had spent hours talking her mother into. They'd almost had a fight over it.

"Why?" Mom had said. "What's wrong with my hair?"

"Nothing," Holly said. "But highlights are cool. They'll make you look younger."

Not the right thing to say.

Mom had gotten all huffy and said that she was as young as she felt and what did Holly know anyway? She was only fifteen, and—

In the end, they compromised.

Mom would get highlights, but she drew the line at a manicure. Holly was itching to tackle Mom's nails but now contented herself with brushing Mom's hair. Something aromatic wafted up.

Holly sniffed.

It smelled suspiciously like the conditioner they used on the horses' manes and tails before a show. Bending closer, Holly sniffed again, just to make sure.

"What's wrong?" Mom said.

"Did you use Show Sheen?"

"Of course not," Mom said and plucked a blue and orange container from her dresser. "I used this. The hairdresser sold it to me."

Holly read the label. "Mom, it's got the same ingredients as Show Sheen and it's three times as expensive."

"You're kidding."

"Nope," Holly said.

"Live and learn," Mom said, reading the label herself. "Just remind me not to use this goop in the barn."

After they got through giggling, Holly finished brushing her mother's hair, then clipped on a silver butterfly surrounded with tiny pink pearls. It was all Mom wanted. Not a veil or flowers—just a tribute to Ben's love of butterflies. Kate said he'd be wearing a tiny silver horseshoe on his lapel. A tear trickled down Mom's cheek.

Was she thinking about Dad?

How did it feel, marrying someone else when you still loved the first person you'd married? Dad had died three years ago and Holly missed him like mad, but she also knew that he'd want Mom to be happy.

And she was—with Kate's father.

They were a perfect match. Ben loved butterflies, Mom loved horses, and they both loved Kate and Holly. It was even better than Holly's favorite movie, *The Parent Trap*, because it was real and it was about to happen.

To them.

"I'm okay," Mom said, patting Holly's hand. "Are you?" She paused. "I mean, are you happy that I'm marrying Ben?"

"Are you kidding? It's—"

"—exactly what you and Kate wanted?"

"Yes." With a sniff, Holly wiped away her own tears and mopped up Mom's damp cheeks. No point in applying blush till they were through feeling weepy.

"I need to feed the horses," Mom said.

Holly shook her head. "Sue and Robin are doing it."

They'd also be at the wedding. But that wasn't until noon, which gave Mom plenty of time to get herself into a minor panic and then out again.

It was a bit weird, seeing Mom close to a meltdown, given how cool she was with difficult horses, including Buccaneer, who'd arrived at the barn last summer all lathered up and snorting like a dragon. He'd almost pulled Mom off her feet. There was a soft knock at the door.

"Coffee?" said Aunt Bea. "For the bride?"

"Come in," Holly said.

Aunt Bea wasn't really her aunt, but the next best thing—Mom's oldest friend—and she'd be staying with them while Mom and Ben were away. She was also Mom's matron of honor, and her special friend Mr. Evans—he'd told the girls to call him Earl—would be Ben's best man. Holly wanted Aunt Bea to marry Mr. Evans but didn't dare meddle like she had with her mom and Kate's dad.

Well, not meddle, exactly. More like pushing them together, gently, whenever possible—like the cooking lessons she and Kate had bought them for Christmas and leaving them alone in the living room with the lights turned low, a bottle of wine, and soft rock on Mom's old stereo.

Holly gave a little sigh.

This was a dream come true. It even took away the sour taste of Mrs. Dean's idiotic plans for the horse camp.

At least it did for a couple of days. On Monday, they'd all
have to face it. But Mom wouldn't. By then she and Ben
would be—where, exactly?

Holly was itching to know.

* * *

Holly had joked about wanting pink unicorns to pull a
gold carriage for their parents' wedding, but they'd had to
settle for Marmalade and an old buggy festooned with
silver ribbons and pink roses from Aunt Marion's garden.
Watched over by Mr. Evans's foreman in the parking lot,
Marmalade dozed contentedly between the shafts while a
stream of guests piled into "Dancing Wings," Dad's butterfly museum.

Way more than Kate had expected.

Peering from the museum's gift shop that they were
using as a dressing room, Kate worried that the place
wouldn't be able to hold them all. It seemed as if most of
Timber Ridge had shown up, including Angela and her
mother.

Mrs. Dean wore black lace, and her hair was pulled
back so tight, it yanked up her eyebrows as if she'd had a
face lift. With a thin-lipped red smile, she glanced around.
The gaudy blush on her cheeks made her look like a
clown.

"Ignore her," Holly said.

Kate gritted her teeth. "I'll try."

It wasn't easy. Ever since Kate arrived at Timber Ridge last summer, Mrs. Dean and Angela had done their best to keep her off the riding team, and they'd succeeded more than once.

But not any more.

After today Kate would be a legal resident of Timber Ridge, and short of firing Liz, there was nothing Mrs. Dean could do about it. And she couldn't spoil this wonderful moment, either.

It belonged to Kate and Holly and their parents.

The ceremony would be held inside the museum's glass atrium amid waterfalls, winding paths, and tropical plants that Kate had never learned the names of. Only the wedding party would be in there so as not stress Dad's rare moths and butterflies. Everyone else would watch Liz and Ben get married from the foyer that Aunt Marion and Mrs. Gordon, Dad's assistant, had decorated with flowers, fairy lights, and tissue paper butterflies in a rainbow of colors.

"It's magic." Holly sighed. "I just love it."

"Me, too," Kate said.

Her discarded jeans hung over Dad's cash register; Holly's baseball cap, sneakers, and socks littered the gift shop's floor. Aunt Bea had zipped them into their bridesmaid's dresses and then disappeared to help Liz.

So far, nobody had seen her gown.

Last night they'd rehearsed their moves, going over

them again and again until Aunt Bea was satisfied. The only one who hadn't rehearsed his role was Marmalade, and he was too sleepy to care. If you wanted him to trot on a Saturday, you had to mention it on Wednesday so he'd have time to get used to the idea.

"Is my hair okay?" Holly said.

They'd just taken turns with a curling iron in the shop's tiny bathroom, laughing and getting in each other's way. Blond ringlets framed Holly's heart-shaped face and cascaded across her shoulders.

Kate shrugged. "You look fine."

"As if you'd know." With a grin, Holly added the finishing touch—a circlet of rosebuds that Aunt Bea had made to match their dresses. She handed the other one to Kate.

"Do I *have* to?"

"Yes."

Kate slapped it onto her head. She hated stuff like this. The dress was bad enough—at least it didn't itch—and she wasn't sure she'd last the whole afternoon in the pink pumps that Holly had made her buy . . . but a tiara of rosebuds?

She felt about five years old.

"Sweet," said Aunt Bea, popping into the room. "Now, Holly, Adam's here and—"

Holly raced for the door.

Aunt Bea held up her hand. "You can't go out there yet. Not till your mother's ready and Ben and Earl are in place."

Kate wondered if Brad had arrived.

Last night at the rehearsal, she'd told Brad about the kidnapping in England, but he'd already known. His sister had filled him in. After that, he'd acted kind of distant. And when they'd walked outside and Kate was hoping for a goodbye kiss, Brad muttered something about having to help his father and had roared off in his truck.

Okay, so what had Sue told him?

Had she made mountains out of molehills and blathered on about Nathan Crane?

But that was crazy.

Kate hadn't even talked to Nathan in England, never mind seen him. Besides, he was now dating Twiggy, which was totally cool. Kate still liked Nathan, but only as a friend.

She liked Brad much better.

He was easy to be with, he didn't have fans screaming for autographs and clawing at his clothes every time he went out in public, and he loved horses as much as Kate did. Maybe Brad was just nervous about the wedding.

Kate certainly was.

Suppose she tripped going down the aisle or let out a gigantic sneeze when her father was about to slip the ring onto Liz's finger. Riding a cross-country course was a whole lot easier than this, and she didn't have to do it wearing pink shoes that wanted to eat her toes.

* * *

Holly almost burst into tears when a pink butterfly landed right next to the silver one she'd pinned into Mom's hair. It really was magic, being a part of all this. The moment Mom said, "I do," Holly shot a sideways glance at Kate, standing beside her.

"Sisters?" Holly whispered.

Kate nodded. "Forever."

The pastor pronounced their parents husband and wife, and then came the kissing bit. Holly felt herself blush. She hadn't seen Mom kiss Kate's dad before. Holding hands, they turned and scooped Kate and Holly into exuberant hugs—probably not part of the ceremony, but who cared at this point?

"We love you guys," Mom said.

She retrieved her bouquet of pink roses from Aunt Bea then took Ben's arm and floated back toward the foyer in her long, creamy gown that Holly still couldn't take her eyes off. When she got married, she wanted a dress just like it, with lace flowers around the neckline and a train and everything.

On each side of the atrium's glass doors, Adam and Brad stood like a pair of sentries. Adam nodded as the wedding party walked past, and a lock of streaky blond hair flopped over his forehead. He flicked it away and grinned at Holly.

She grinned back.

It wasn't often she got to see Adam all dressed up.

Well, except at horse shows when he pretty much wore the same clothes she did—black hunt jacket, buff breeches, helmet, and a white shirt. Otherwise he slouched about in jeans and t-shirts. His favorite was the one that Holly had given him for his birthday, and he was even brave enough to wear it at his barn. On the front it said—

Dressage riders are letter perfect!

He got teased a lot and didn't care—like right now. Some guys wouldn't be caught dead wearing a pink tie. Adam just shrugged it off, the way he always did, and Holly couldn't wait for the music to begin so they could dance together.

But first came the receiving line.

A whole bunch of people Holly didn't even know shook Mom's hand and clucked over how grown-up Holly was. A couple of Ben's old classmates were there, and so was Angela's former stepfather, Henry Dean, with sweet little Marcia clinging to his hand. She'd be staying with her best friend, Laura Gardner, for the horse camp.

Holly snuck a glance at Angela.

She hadn't even bothered to get in line. Neither had her mother. She was bending someone's ear at the buffet table, a reporter from the looks of it. The man wore an earnest expression and clutched an iPad that he was tapping on furiously in time with Mrs. Dean's lipsticked mouth.

What idiocy was Mrs. Dean up to now?

Last year, she'd hired a photographer to take publicity shots of Angela in a classical dressage outfit—shadbelly, top hat, and yellow vest—that she posted on the barn's Facebook page and made everyone cringe. Angela could barely manage a first-level test, never mind anything higher. Then came a ruthless trainer who zapped Angela's horse with electrified poles.

Mom had tossed him out.

But Mrs. Dean didn't care. She acted as if nothing untoward had happened and promptly dragged Angela off to join a competing team. At the next show, Timber Ridge beat them soundly, and a few weeks later Angela returned to the barn, not the least bit embarrassed about her foolish mother.

4

To Kate's relief, the line of well-wishers finally fizzled out, and Liz and Dad—still holding hands—were propelled outside, where Marmalade waited with his flowery coach. Dad helped Liz on board and climbed in after her. They settled into their seats beneath a bower of pink roses. Petals drifted down.

"Smile," Holly said, aiming her cell phone.

Liz took the reins and everyone cheered as the barn's biggest horse hauled them out of the parking lot and down Main Street, where strangers stopped to wave and shout congratulations. Someone—probably Aunt Bea—had hung a sign on the back of the buggy that said:

Just married.

Good old Marmalade trundled back to the museum,

not the least bit fazed by the streamers and balloons that trailed in his wake. One popped and he didn't even flinch.

"You're way better than a unicorn," Kate said kissing his chestnut nose.

A ribbon dangled loose, so Kate retied it to Marmalade's harness which she and Holly had decorated the night before. They'd spent hours cleaning and oiling it, and then weaving pink and silver ribbons along the reins and traces. Holly had even added tiny pink pom-poms to Marmalade's bridle. Kate thought it was a bit over the top, but he didn't seem to mind.

The photographer, who'd been setting up his equipment in the foyer, ordered everyone back inside. He was lining up his first shot of the wedding party when something caught Kate's eye.

She turned and saw Angela at the buffet table scooping strawberry punch into a couple of glasses. Her best friend, Kristina James, gave Angela a high five as if they'd just sealed a stupendous deal.

It happened fast.

One moment Angela and Kristina were sauntering past the wedding party, drinks in hand. The next, a cloud of pink cascaded down the front of Liz's dress.

"Oops, sorry," Angela said, not sounding sorry at all.

"You did that on purpose," Holly yelled.

Angela shrugged. "I tripped."

Fists clenched, Holly looked ready to tear Angela

apart. Kate held her back while Aunt Bea calmed everyone down by saying she could fix it.

But how?

Liz's gorgeous dress was ruined, and the photographer was having a hissy fit because he hadn't taken any pictures yet. By this time, Angela and Kristina had conveniently disappeared. So had Mrs. Dean.

"Good riddance," Holly muttered.

"Get my sewing basket," Aunt Bea said and sent Holly scurrying for the gift shop. "Kate, tell that DJ to keep everyone amused."

"What can I do to help?" said Mr. Evans.

Teach Angela some manners?

Last winter Angela had called Mr. Evans a freak because of his birthmark. It covered half his face, curved around one ear, and ran across the top of his shiny bald head like a map of Indonesia. He'd brushed off Angela's rudeness with a friendly smile, but Kate knew it had hurt him.

She shot him a knowing look, then raced off to give the DJ his orders. By the time she got back, the DJ had already launched into a round of wedding jokes and Aunt Bea was fixing Liz's dress. Skillfully, she wrapped Liz's train to the front, draped it over the skirt's ugly stain, and made a few quick stitches to hold it in place.

"It's not perfect," she declared. "But it'll do."

"Thank you," Liz said. "You're a life saver."

"I can fix it," Holly said. "In Photoshop."

"Yes, but not right now," Aunt Bea said. "Okay, places everyone. We've got pictures to take and a party to enjoy."

* * *

First to dance was the wedding couple, followed by Aunt Bea and Mr. Evans, looking smooth enough to be on *Dancing with the Stars*. Kate glanced at Brad. Was he dreading his obligatory dance with her? He still hadn't said more than a few words since the whole thing began.

"Okay, folks," sang out the DJ. "Now, let's welcome our absolutely stunning bridesmaids and their handsome escorts onto the floor."

Everyone applauded and Kate blushed. If they ever invented a button that would stop blushes from happening, she'd be first in line to buy it.

Brad held her at arm's length.

Kate looked to the side and saw Holly dancing almost cheek-to-cheek with Adam. So were Dad and Liz, completely wrapped up in each other. Even Aunt Bea and Mr. Evans looked quite cozy as they wafted by. Brad trod on Kate's foot.

"Sorry," he muttered.

"It's okay," Kate said, wishing she didn't feel so awkward.

It wasn't like this before she went to England. They hadn't exactly gone on dates, not like to the movies or even out for pizza but they'd skied together and Brad had driven her to physical therapy every day after she injured her knee. He'd also cheered her on at horse shows and kissed her when she won a ribbon at the Festival of Horses.

Kate plucked up her courage. "I'm not dating Nathan."

"If you say so."

Oh, great. So what did that mean?

The DJ switched tracks. Drums thumped and guitars wailed, and Kate couldn't even hear herself think. Whatever she said now would be drowned out by Lady Gaga. Someone tapped on her shoulder.

"My turn," said Kristina James.

* * *

Holly hauled Kate into the gift shop because she wanted to fix her makeup. Kate didn't give a toss about hers. Who cared if her cheeks were flushed or her eye shadow had smudged? And she couldn't wait to scrape it all off, either. Everyone else was still dancing, including Brad and Kristina. Well, not exactly dancing. More like draping themselves over one another.

"It's Adam's fault," Holly said, dragging a brush through her hair so hard that Aunt Bea's rosebud tiara slipped sideways. She yanked it off.

Kate removed hers and laid it gently on the counter. A pink petal floated to the floor. "Why?"

"Because he told Brad."

"No, it was Sue," Kate said. "Remember our trail ride? She was convinced I'd gone back to Nathan, no matter what I said. I had the feeling she couldn't wait to tell Brad."

"Okay, yeah," Holly said. "But Adam embellished it. He put the whole kidnapping story on his Facebook page—like *every* last detail—and made it sound like you were involved."

"But I was."

"Yes, but not with Nathan. You helped rescue Adam and Twiggy, but you didn't even see Nathan in England, remember?" Holly pursed her lips and swiped on another layer of gloss. She whirled around. "You don't care about him any more, do you?"

"You *know* I don't."

Holly held up her hands. "Just asking."

"Well, I don't," Kate said. "He's just a friend."

"That's what I told Adam," Holly said. "But he didn't listen, as usual." She took a deep breath. "I'm sorry Brad's being a jerk."

"Yeah, me, too." Kate looked longingly at her jeans, still hanging over Dad's cash register. Would anyone notice—or even care—if she slipped into them and rode back to the barn with Marmalade?

Her arms ached to hug Tapestry and Magician because they would understand. They'd listen and nod their heads, and she would feed them carrots and bury her face in their manes and breathe in their horsey smells. She'd—

"Don't even think about it," Holly said.

"What?"

"Going to the barn."

Kate stared at her. "How did you know?"

"Because you've got that *I've gotta hug my horse* look on your face."

That was the trouble. Holly knew her so well that Kate couldn't get away with anything.

Would it always be like this?

They were both only children—used to being by themselves—and now they were sisters. They'd be living under each other's feet and sharing a bedroom for the next three years until they went off to college.

Kate wanted to study math and biology; Holly favored art and theater. There was little chance they'd end up at the same school. Would they drift apart then?

Kate didn't want to think about it.

"So what are we gonna do about Angela?" Holly said twisting her hair into a knot and letting it go. "She wrecked Mom's dress, and I won't let her get away with it."

"But she always does," Kate said. "When's the last time Angela got in trouble?"

Holly scowled. "Like *never*."

"I wish Jennifer was here," Kate said. "She'd think of something."

"Yeah," Holly said. "And it'd probably backfire."

Kate thought for a minute. "Look," she said, "the only way to beat Angela is to *beat her in public*, like at a—"

"—horse show?" Holly said.

"Yes."

"But we already *do* that," Holly said. "No, this time I want it to be different. I want to make Angela squirm in front of everyone. I want to make her look like a total jerk."

"So tell Brad to give her lessons."

Holly snorted. "C'mon," she said, grinning. "Let's get back or we'll miss Mom shoving cake into your dad's face."

"Ugh," Kate said. "Do they *have* to?"

"Yes, it's tradition."

Reluctantly, Kate followed Holly back into the noise and bustle of their parents' wedding. Brad was now dancing with Angela, and at their table—talking a mile a minute with Mrs. Dean—was a young woman Kate didn't know. She had long, auburn hair and a pale face with so many freckles it made her look as if she'd spent way too much time in the sun.

Was that Jocelyn Fraser, the ditzy trainer from Larchwood who'd be taking over while Liz was away?

"She's a bobblehead," Holly said.

Despite herself, Kate laughed. The woman was nodding at Angela's mother like a plastic toy on the dashboard of a muscle car.

* * *

An hour later, they cut the cake. Kate's father tried to stuff a piece into Liz's mouth, but she fended him off and shoved a messy chunk into his mouth instead.

"Go, Mom," Holly yelled.

On the count of three, Liz tossed her bouquet. Ribbons trailing like a kite, it sailed into the air, and dozens of eager hands reached upward.

Kate held her breath.

She wanted Holly to catch it, but Kristina shoved them both to one side and snagged Liz's pink roses for herself. With a sly smile, she threw the bouquet to Brad and blew him a kiss.

"N-i-c-e," Angela drawled.

Gritting her teeth, Kate turned away. Angela had a lot of nerve, opening her mouth after what she'd done to Liz's beautiful dress. But now wasn't the time to pick a fight. That would have to wait until later, after Liz and Dad had gone.

Kate still had no idea what, if anything, they could do to make Angela pay, but there had to be something.

As if reading her mind, Holly said, "We'll figure it out."

5

AMID A FLURRY OF LOST WALLETS, misplaced passports, and endless hugs, Ben and Mom finally left for the airport at nine on Sunday morning. The moment they drove off, Holly rounded on Kate.

"Okay, where are they going?"

"Austria."

Holly thought for a minute. While geography wasn't her best subject, she pretty much knew where Austria was, but only because of Vienna and its world-famous Lipizzaner stallions. "You mean the Spanish Riding School?"

"Yup, and Dad's going to take her."

"More like *she* will take *him*," Holly said, grinning.

After Kate had explained about her father's butterfly lecture tour with the University of Vienna, Holly wondered if Mom had packed her breeches and dressage boots.

But that was a pipe dream.

No way would the riding school let Mom ride one of their horses, never mind she was so talented she could ride a cow side-saddle over a four-foot fence and win a blue ribbon doing it. She'd be treated like any other tourist, unless Ben had convinced the university to pull strings. Maybe they'd get special seating at a performance or be given a private tour of the stables. But there wasn't time to worry about that. Horse camp would start tomorrow and already kids and ponies had begun to arrive.

All at once, it seemed.

With Robin's help, Holly and Kate did the best they could. There wouldn't be enough stalls in the main barn to house the newcomers, so they shifted Marmalade and the ponies to the rebuilt upper barn—something else that had changed while they were in England.

"Where's Sue?" Holly said, leading a reluctant Plug into his new stall. "Why isn't she here?" Sue always pitched in with chores, no matter what needed to be done.

Robin shrugged. "She's helping her parents pack."

"Are they going on vacation?"

"No, they're moving."

There was a stunned silence. Holly looked at Robin like she'd just sprouted wings and a tail. "You're kidding."

"I wish I was."

"What happened?" Kate said.

"Mrs. Dean has hired someone else to run the ski

area," Robin said and burst into tears. Holly fished in her pocket and found a clean tissue. She handed it to Robin, now leaning against Daisy's black-and-white shoulder. The mare grunted but didn't move.

"I thought the Pirettis owned it."

"They did," Robin said. "But things got kind of difficult, and a whole lot went wrong. Sue said her parents were fighting about money all the time. So when Mrs. Dean offered to buy them out, they grabbed it." There was a lengthy pause while Robin blew her nose. "I just found out that Sue's moving to Colorado. Her father has a new job at Vail."

"Is that a ski area?" Holly said.

"A huge one." Robin wiped her eyes. "And it's got a fabulous snowboarding program, so Brad will be happy."

"Why didn't Sue tell us?" Kate said.

"Because it's been very hush-hush and nobody was allowed to say a word."

Holly tried to process all this.

Sue's family was as much a part of Vermont as fall foliage, maple syrup, and Ben & Jerry's ice cream. Mr. and Mrs. Piretti had run the ski lodge forever, Brad was the high school's star quarterback, and Sue—well, she'd been a Timber Ridge rider ever since she and Holly had ridden their shaggy ponies together in lead-line classes.

No wonder Brad had acted so weird yesterday. It had nothing to do with his stupid suspicions about Kate and

Nathan—it was all about him moving and being too chicken to break Mrs. Dean's idiotic rule and tell Kate about it.

Boys.

They could be such cowards.

* * *

Kids and ponies crowded the barn's parking lot. Kate counted twice. There were only five new campers, but with all the confusion, it felt more like fifty. Trailers backed into the wrong spots, parents yelled at their children, and Dr. Fleming showed up to vet-check the new arrivals. Someone's dog shot between a pony's hind legs and almost got trampled.

This was worse than a horse show.

All of a sudden, Kate felt a pang of sympathy for show secretaries when hordes of riders descended all at once, demanding numbers and schedules and complaining about the stalls they were given.

Thank goodness for Marcia and Laura.

Like junior goodwill ambassadors, they mingled with the new kids and told them how fabulous Timber Ridge was. It added to the chaos, but at least nobody was complaining.

Until Mrs. Dean showed up.

She arrived in her Mercedes and slammed on the brakes, scaring a bay pony that had just been unloaded.

Waving her stick-thin arms, Angela's mother stepped from her car and scared even more ponies. Tails flagged and nostrils flaring, they skittered about and eyed their new surroundings with suspicion. So did the kids.

One of them said, "Is she a witch?"

As usual Mrs. Dean was dressed in black, never mind it was mid-summer and blisteringly hot. She staggered about in pointed-toe boots with three-inch heels, a fringed leather vest, and tight black pants that made her skinny bowed legs look as if she'd spent years in the saddle.

"The Timber Ridge cowboy," Holly muttered.

Biting back a grin, Kate consulted her list. Names blurred and ran together as she handed out the tags that Holly had made—Nadine, Amber, Gabrielle, Maeve, and Eden. She'd worry about matching up their last names later.

Five girls and five ponies.

Check.

But Mrs. Dean had her own list. One by one, she called out names and whisked the new kids away to the families they'd be staying with. Her car was big enough to hold all of them.

"So who's gonna take care of their ponies?" Holly said.

Kate shrugged. "Us, I guess."

Moments after they settled the new arrivals into their stalls, a Range Rover pulled up. Its back door opened and a little girl climbed out. She didn't look much older than eight, but Kate knew that you had to be at least ten to be part of the Timber Ridge camp. Hands shoved into both pockets, the girl didn't look up until Holly said, "What's your name."

"Charlotte." The girl hesitated. "Baker."

Kate looked at her list again. The only unclaimed pony was the Norwegian Fjord, so it had to belong to Charlotte. Just to make sure, Kate said, "What's your pony's name?"

"Elke."

"Summer Solstice?"

"Yes." The little girl reached for her braid—long and brown and extremely neat—that hung to her waist. She stuck the tip into her mouth and chewed for a few seconds, then spat it out. "But we only use that for shows."

But what kind of shows? That sweet Norwegian Fjord couldn't hold a candle to the highly polished ponies that now filled the barn. Some of them, Kate knew from articles in the *Chronicle*, cost a small fortune.

"So, Charlie," Holly said. "Let's go and see your pony."

"She's *not* a pony, and my name is *not* Charlie," the girl said, digging her heels into the dirt and creating a minor dust storm. "It's Charlotte."

"Oh, sorry," Holly said.

Kate grinned at her. "I think you've just been told off."

* * *

For the tenth time in as many minutes Kate checked her watch. It was nine thirty on Monday morning, and that ditzy trainer Mrs. Dean had hired hadn't even shown up yet. She was supposed to have been there at eight.

The barn was in an uproar.

Half the camp kids didn't know how to tack up their horses; the other half complained about having to clean stalls. Even Charlotte Baker was having a hard time, but at least she was trying. With an almighty shove, she pushed Elke to one side so there'd be room in her stall for the muck bucket—not that she knew what to do with it. Most of the manure she lobbed into it missed the mark. The only ones getting on with the job were Laura Gardner and Marcia Dean.

Holly pulled a face. "Chaos."

"No kidding," Kate said.

Deftly, she dodged a loose pony and caught another by its dangling lead rope. The aisle echoed with hooves. Kids shouted. One of them—her nametag said Nadine Webb—was putting her gelding's bridle on backward. He shook his handsome bay head and spat out the bit. Kate was about to help when Marcia Dean took over.

"Thanks," Kate said.

Marcia didn't have her own pony and she'd already outgrown Plug, so for the camp sessions she'd be riding Daisy. Trouble was, she'd outgrown Daisy as well, not in size, because Marcia was petite, but in ability. Last year,

Kate had let her ride Tapestry and she'd done amazingly well.

Kate frowned and thought for a moment. Jennifer had asked her to exercise Rebel, which wouldn't leave her much time to ride Tapestry now that camp had begun. From the way things were going, she'd be too busy helping kids, especially since Jocelyn Fraser still hadn't made an appearance. Holly was worried that if the camp experiment didn't work out, Mrs. Dean would blame Liz, even though she wasn't even around, which meant Kate and Holly had to pitch in whether or not they wanted to.

So maybe, just maybe . . .

"Hey, Marcia," Kate said quietly so nobody else could hear. "Come with me."

She pulled Marcia into Tapestry's stall. Almost immediately, Marcia wrapped her arms around Tapestry's copper-colored neck and hung on like a limpet. Tapestry vacuumed up another bit of hay from the ground, then raised her head and lifted Marcia off her feet.

"That was fun," Marcia squealed. "Let's do it again."

"No time," Kate said, detaching Marcia from Tapestry. She turned her around. The little girl's brown eyes looked huge in her freckled face. Nerves or expectations? Kate couldn't tell.

"Do you want to ride Tapestry?" she said.

Marcia swallowed hard. "Like, right now?"

"Yes," Kate said. "Instead of Daisy."

This might turn into a huge mistake, but Kate wanted Marcia to do well and feel good about herself. According to the camp schedule, there'd be trail rides, a scavenger hunt, and a horse show with ribbons and a special prize for the rider who got the most points.

Marcia had never won a ribbon.

Before moving to New York with her father last Halloween, Marcia had lived at Timber Ridge under Angela's malevolent shadow. She'd been a real-life Cinderella who cleaned tack and groomed her elder stepsister's expensive horse that Angela didn't give two figs about. And now, here was a chance for Marcia to shine, to show Mrs. Dean, her former stepmother, that she was worth something. Kate was determined to make it happen.

But riding dear old Daisy wouldn't cut it.

No way could Marcia compete with the other kids. Their sleek hunter-jumpers were more like miniature Thoroughbreds than ordinary ponies, including Laura Gardner's cute little chestnut, Soupçon, who'd arrived at the barn six months before.

"Wow," Marcia said. "Do you mean it?"

"Yes," Kate said and hoped Holly wouldn't have a meltdown. For some odd reason she'd been critical about Kate letting Marcia ride Tapestry last year.

But it had worked out fine.

Marcia had even learned how to make Tapestry lie down on command, a trick that Kate had taught her, much to the delight of the barn's younger crowd. They loved watching Tapestry's knees buckle, and then her hindquarters as she collapsed in a heap with a big sigh, as if to say, "Why are we doing this again?"

Holly didn't always get it.

She'd always had her own horse, thanks to Liz's job at the stables, so she didn't understand what it was like to be in a barn full of kids with their own ponies while you were stuck with the ones that nobody else wanted, or even dared, to ride.

Like Buccaneer.

Was he missing her in England? Did he even care that Kate was no longer there? Did he miss the Life Savers, the carrots, and the hours she'd spent brushing and hugging him? Pulling her scattered thoughts together, Kate watched Marcia groom Tapestry and wondered why Mr. Dean didn't buy his horse-crazy daughter a pony.

He could easily afford it.

Perhaps it was because they lived in Manhattan. Marcia hid her disappointment by joking about it. She told Kate they weren't allowed to have pets in their apartment.

"Except for fish," she explained, brushing Tapestry so vigorously that she snorted and moved sideways. "You can have a pet as long as it lives underwater."

"Frogs?" Kate suggested.

Marcia nodded, then shot Kate a sly grin. "Yes, but I have a hamster instead. His name is Geoffrey."

"But—" Kate began.

"It's legal," Marcia said, grinning even wider. "Because he's *under water*."

Visions of hamsters with snorkels and tiny fins swam into view. "How did you manage that?" Kate said.

Marcia rolled her eyes as if the answer were obvious and Kate was too dumb to see it. "Easy peasy," she said. "I put a glass of water on top of Geoffrey's cage."

"Sweet," Kate said, doubling up with laughter. She couldn't wait to tell Holly about this one.

6

STANDING AT THE RAIL, Kate kept an anxious eye on her horse as eight little girls trotted around Jocelyn Fraser in the outdoor ring. So far, Marcia and Tapestry were doing a fine job. So were Laura and Soupy, but the others weren't.

Holly groaned. "Doesn't look good."

"I know," Kate said.

Despite their glossy ponies and designer jods, the camp kids were all over the place. Nadine posted on the wrong diagonal, and Gabrielle's pony, Sandcastle, kept trying to take a chunk out of Elke's well-rounded rump. The Fjord sidestepped just in time, but poor Charlotte almost fell off. Then Amber lost her stirrups, and Maeve's pinto got the bit between her teeth and took off at a brisk canter, crashing into Eden's roan gelding.

The barn's new instructor paid no attention. Miss Picture Perfect was too busy texting and didn't even bother to look up when Mrs. Dean's silver Mercedes rolled into the parking lot. Angela jumped out, followed by Kristina. They wore spotless polo shirts and baby blue breeches—not exactly the best clothes for barn chores.

"Nice of them to show up," Kate said.

They were supposed to be helping, but so far she and Holly had done all the work. Robin was at the Pirettis' house. She was going with them to Colorado for a couple of weeks, which meant she wouldn't be around to help, either.

Kate kept a wary lookout for Brad. She hadn't seen him since the wedding. No texts, no calls. And it stung—more than she wanted to admit—because it left her with the uncomfortable feeling that she was part of the problem.

No, wait a minute.

This was Brad's problem, not hers. If he didn't believe her, well too bad. But even if she *had* seen Nathan in London, so what? She wasn't actually dating Brad, so he didn't have any right to get on his high horse about it. Something hot surged up her throat. She swallowed hard, and it tasted bitter.

Anger?

Okay, so who was she angry at? Brad for being a jerk or herself for letting him walk all over her? Whatever it was, Kate was through with the whole guy thing. They were a distraction she couldn't afford . . . well, until the right one came along.

* * *

Aunt Bea had left egg salad sandwiches and a plate of cookies on the kitchen table. Tucked beneath the salt-shaker was a note that said:

> *Am writing. Do not disturb unless house on fire or George Clooney calls.*

Kate ginned. Aunt Bea wrote mysteries for a living, and the minute Liz's wedding was over she'd swapped her sewing machine for her laptop and locked herself in the guest room, racing to meet her publisher's deadline, which she said was so tight it squeaked.

After scarfing down lunch, the girls raced back to the barn. Holly zoomed into the tack room and announced she was going for a trail ride. "Are you coming with me?"

"But what about the kids?"

"Let Princess Angela and Lady Kristina deal with them," Holly said, yanking Magician's saddle off its peg. She snatched up his bridle and whipped around so fast, its reins slapped into Kate's shoulder. "Well?"

"Yeah, I guess."

So far, neither Angela nor Kristina had lifted a finger to help, except for escorting the campers to a gourmet lunch at the club. No PBJs or cold pizza for these precious kids. They were being primed—maybe even bribed—to persuade their parents to buy houses at Timber Ridge so that Mrs. Dean could turn it into a playground for the rich.

As if it weren't already rich enough.

"Just because your father married Liz doesn't mean you're back on the riding team," Angela had told Kate, shortly before she and Kristina sauntered off with the camp kids.

Holly snorted. "In your dreams."

"What*ever*." Angela shrugged. "But don't say I didn't warn you."

An hour later, it still rankled. Kate shook her head as she groomed and tacked up Rebel. This was ridiculous, letting Angela get to her like this. From now on she would ignore her.

"Can I come with you?" said a small voice.

Another chimed in. "Me, too."

Startled, Kate turned to find Marcia and Charlotte looking at her through the bars of Rebel's stall. They both switched on such high-wattage smiles, Kate couldn't resist.

"Okay, sure," she said.

In a flash, Holly strode across the aisle. "Don't be an idiot," she said under her breath. "Mrs. Dean will have a bird if we take off with her precious campers."

"I doubt it," Kate said.

Mrs. Dean didn't care a hoot about her former stepdaughter. She wasn't trying to lure Marcia and her father back to Timber Ridge. The only reason Marcia was in the camp program was because Laura Gardner had invited her. Not that Laura needed to be at camp either, given that she already lived here. But her parents had pots of money and a ton of influential friends. That was the market Mrs. Dean planned to exploit, according to Aunt Bea.

And she was rarely wrong.

Not about conspiracies, anyway. Aunt Bea had a nose like Sherlock Holmes and the determination of a bulldog. When Magician disappeared last summer, she'd organized the search party with the efficiency of a Marine drill sergeant.

"Please," said Marcia.

Holly scowled. "Oh, all right, but if you get in trouble—"

"We won't," Charlotte said. "And Laura will come, too."

"What are you supposed to be doing this afternoon?" Kate said as she helped Marcia with Tapestry. It felt odd, getting her horse ready for someone else to ride.

"Swimming lessons," Charlotte said from Elke's stall. "I already know how to swim. I want to ride." There was a pause. "My father says I'm not good enough and that I have to practice."

"We all have to practice," Kate told her. "Even Charlotte Dujardin."

Charlotte's blue-green eyes popped wide open. "*Char-lotte*?" she squeaked as if she'd never heard of anyone else having her name before.

"Yes," Kate said. "She's the best dressage rider in the world."

"What's dressage?"

"Something you need to practice." Kate tightened Tapestry's girth then handed the reins to Marcia. "Take her outside. I'll give you a leg-up."

Holly whipped out her cell phone. "Guess I'd better call Mrs. Dean, huh?"

"Earth to witch," Kate said without thinking.

The girls giggled.

"Forget I said that," Kate warned.

Mrs. Dean wouldn't care about Marcia and Laura blowing off their swimming lessons, but if Charlotte Baker was a prize catch, there would be trouble later.

* * *

With Charlotte riding beside her, Kate learned that Charlotte's parents were divorced and that her mother—who knew zilch about horses—had bought Elke as a birthday gift for Charlotte three months before.

"That's awesome," Kate said, meaning it. What little girl wouldn't want a pony for her birthday?

Awkwardly, Charlotte flung her arms around Elke's

chunky neck. "She's the best horse in the world, but Dad—"

"What?"

"Nothing," Charlotte said.

The Fjord ambled along the trail and didn't even spook when a squirrel shot across their path. Kate had a hard time keeping Rebel under control. Jennifer's horse snorted and whirled around, bumping into Elke's shoulder. She didn't even twitch.

Talk about bombproof.

But there was something about the way Charlotte rode that made Kate wince. The girl didn't seem comfortable, even though Elke was just walking. Charlotte's hands were stiff and her feet were jammed so far into the stirrups that she'd probably get dragged if she fell off. Kate bent down to adjust them.

"Like this," she said. "On the balls of your feet. Heels down, toes up." She patted Charlotte's knee. *"Hielen omlaag."*

"What's that?"

"It's Dutch for *heels down,*" Kate said.

Sounding slightly awed, Charlotte said, "Do you talk Dutch?"

"No. I read it in a time-travel book about a girl who loves horses." Kate paused. "I don't even know if I'm saying it right."

"Can I read it?"

"Sure," Kate said, "if I can find it." Half her stuff was still at her aunt's cottage in the village.

Ahead, music erupted.

Holly's cell phone? She was always changing the ring tone and Kate hadn't heard this one before. It was probably Mrs. Dean, calling to complain about them taking off with her precious campers.

"It's Twiggy," Holly yelled over her shoulder.

Marcia trotted up. "Who's that?"

"A princess," Kate said.

Questions tumbled out. Soupy shied at a rock, and Laura had such a hard time talking that she was almost speechless.

"A *princess*?"

"For real?" Charlotte said.

"They're a dime a dozen in England," Kate said.

This wasn't quite true, but it would help diffuse the girls' excitement. Twiggy DuBois was, in her own words, a *nothing princess*. Her real name was Princess Isabel of Lunaberg—a tiny country that no longer existed—but she only used her royal title for the fancy occasions she was forced to attend.

The last time Kate had seen Twiggy, she was stranded in an English hospital bed, reconnecting with her critical father and complaining that she didn't really need to be there. To her, the kidnapping adventure had been a huge lark.

Typical Twiggy.

If only she could fly over here and hang out with them at Timber Ridge. That would be the best fun in the world.

But it would never happen.

Prince Ferdinand, Twiggy's father, would never allow her to come. She'd had a hard enough time persuading him that she needed to take riding lessons at Beaumont Park this summer, never mind traveling all the way to Vermont by herself.

Urging Rebel along the narrow trail, Kate ducked a low-hanging branch and drew level with Holly. "What did Twiggy say?"

"Nothing much."

"C'mon," Kate said. "Spill."

Was it her imagination or was Holly being secretive about Twiggy like she had been in England? It had caused a big fight and lots of tears, but somehow they'd patched things up. They were sisters now. They wouldn't have secrets from one another.

Would they?

Holly dropped the phone into her pocket. In a fake British accent, she said, "Princess Twiggy is having a jolly good time at Beaumont Park, Will Hunter is still totes hot, and Diamond is positively brill."

"Cool," Kate said, because Twiggy's old horse, Gemini, had scared her to death, thanks to his evil trainer, Vincent King, who'd almost ruined Buccaneer as well.

Were there laws to stop someone like him?

Kate had no idea. All she knew was that four years ago, Victor Kavanaugh's show jumping career in Europe had turned sour when he'd abused a horse in public. So he'd gone to ground and reinvented himself as Vincent King on this side of the Atlantic. When things went sour here as well, he'd vanished and resurfaced back in England.

Kate shuddered.

Who knew where Vincent King would turn up next?

* * *

"Wow," Holly said when they emerged from the woods. "Take a look at *that*."

Kate held up a hand to shield her eyes from the sun. Ahead was the hunt course—a large, open meadow bordered by hedges, trees, and a stone wall, with jumps scattered around the perimeter and a line of jumps down the middle. Just like always.

Except . . .

All the jumps had been rebuilt—new logs, panels, and rails, along with fresh brush. And where there'd been one jump, there were now two, side-by-side, only one was normal height and the other much lower.

"Nice," Kate said.

The new fences were perfect for younger kids—no higher than two feet—and some had wings to keep the ponies from running out. Had Mrs. Dean engineered this as well?

"Kate, can I jump?" Laura said. "Can I, can I?"

"*May* I," Kate corrected, then nodded.

Laura pointed her chestnut pony at the crossrail. Soupçon tucked his front legs and popped over the jump like the little showboat he was. Wearing a big grin, Laura trotted back. Soupy snorted and flicked his tail as if he wanted everyone to look at him. He gave a little buck.

"Show off," Kate said and smiled.

She'd loved this feisty red pony from the beginning and he was perfect for Laura. She was one of Timber Ridge's up-and-coming stars. Next year, she'd be on the riding team for sure.

"My turn," Marcia said. "Pleeeeze."

"All right," Kate said. "But let me get the kinks out of Tapestry first." Apart from that trail ride last week, she hadn't been ridden in more than a month and would probably race the fences. Or worse, she'd get really frisky and send Marcia flying.

Pulling a fake sad face, Marcia slid off Tapestry, took Rebel's reins from Kate, and held onto both horses while Kate vaulted into the saddle. The stirrups hung six inches above her ankle, and she was tempted to ride without them, but that would be pushing her luck.

Holly breezed past.

She'd already jumped the course and was about to take it again. "Let's do it together," she said.

Kate adjusted her stirrups. "Okay."

They rode the fences side-by-side, taking turns over the different heights. The last jump didn't have wings, so they reached out and held hands. The kids cheered and clapped, and Marcia was all smiles when she got back onto Tapestry.

"Just the low ones," Kate warned as she shortened the stirrups. "Promise?"

Marcia was a gutsy kid. Last fall she'd taken off with her stepsister's horse to prove to Mrs. Dean that she could ride as well as Angela. But she'd gotten caught in a freak blizzard and wound up huddled beneath a jump—right here on the hunt course—and would've frozen to death if Kate and Holly hadn't found her.

"O-*kay*," Marcia said.

She gathered up her reins, and Kate felt a lump in her throat as she watched Tapestry taking such good care of her young rider. Over the fences they went like a couple of pros who'd been doing it forever.

Kate turned to Charlotte, now chewing the end of her braid. "Do you want to jump?" Elke was big enough to step over the low ones.

Charlotte spat out her braid.. "No, thank you."

"Oh, all right," Kate said.

If Charlotte didn't want to jump, that was fine, and it was a good thing she knew her comfort level. Too many kids these days were pushed beyond their limits by parents who lived through their children the way Mrs. Dean did with Angela.

As if on cue, she cantered up.

Specks of foam flew from Ragtime's mouth; his bay shoulders gleamed with sweat. If Kate didn't know better, she'd have thought Angela had been jumping the cross-country course. But she never did that unless there was an audience or she had something to prove, like the race she'd had with Kate last summer. It had almost cost Kate her job at Timber Ridge.

"You're in big trouble," Angela said, glaring at Kate.

"Who says?"

"My mother."

"So who died and left her in charge?" Holly snapped.

Angela smirked. "She's always been in charge. Haven't you figured that out yet?"

"Okay, let her rip," came a man's voice.

Engines roared into life. Beyond the hedge, two bucket loaders reared up, dirt and rocks dripping from their metal jaws like dinosaurs in a cartoon.

"What are they doing?" Kate said, patting Rebel's neck. His ears were pricked so far forward, they almost popped off his face.

"Building an alpine slide."

"Why?"

"Because my mother says so," Angela said sounding less than convinced. She refused to meet Kate in the eye. "It'll be good for Timber Ridge. Everyone knows that."

"Like who?" Holly said.

Angela shrugged. "A couple of state senators, the governor—"

"You have *got* to be kidding," Kate said.

Last she knew, the governor of Vermont was all about conservation. And now, here was Mrs. Dean turning Timber Ridge into an amusement park. Pretty soon they'd have carousels, cotton-candy stands, and a roller coaster. Kate loved carnivals, but not at Timber Ridge, not in the middle of a protected wilderness. At least, Kate thought it was protected. She'd have to ask her father.

"What about the birds, the animals—?" Holly said.

Her voice trailed off, but Kate knew what Holly was thinking. This side of the mountain was home to whip-poorwills, sedge wrens, and a couple of rare bats that were on the endangered list. Kate knew this because her father had drummed it into her. If you mess with their environment, they'll eventually go extinct.

"Who cares about stupid birds?" Angela raked Ragtime's sweaty sides with her spurs and took off.

7

As they rode back to the barn Kate couldn't get her mind off Mrs. Dean's latest scheme. Building an alpine slide next to the Timber Ridge hunt course was totally crazy. The minute one of those carts went zooming down the concrete chute, wheels clacking and kids screaming, the horses would go ballistic. Even stodgy old Marmalade would turn himself inside out. There had to be a way to stop it.

But how?

Charlotte said, "My brother took me to an alpine slide. I fell off."

"Did you get hurt?" Kate said.

"Yeah." Charlotte grimaced. "My legs got all scraped up, and I couldn't ride."

"What about your brother?"

"He didn't get hurt."

"No, I mean does he ride?"

"Yes."

Kate waited for her to go on, but Charlotte clammed up as if a blind had just come down. Did her brother live with her and her mom, or had he gone with his dad? Or maybe he was in college. All Charlotte had said was that her parents weren't together any more. This was tough for a ten-year-old who didn't look any older than eight.

* * *

There was no sign of Angela or her mother when Kate led Rebel into his stall. After helping Marcia with Tapestry, she cornered Holly in the tack room. But all it took was one look at Holly's face and Kate knew they were on the same page. She didn't even need to explain.

"The whippoorwills," Holly said. She slammed her saddle onto its wooden rack so hard that it almost broke. "They're on Vermont's endangered list."

"So are spotted salamanders," Kate said, thinking hard. They couldn't fight Mrs. Dean on their own. "We need to get other people involved."

"How?"

"By showing them what's happening. We'll make posters of cute animals," Kate said. "Something they can recognize and identify with."

"Like a chipmunk?"

"Yes, and squirrels."

"They're not endangered," Holly said. "Most people think squirrels are pests. We need something cute and fuzzy."

"That lets out salamanders."

"What about a fox?"

"That won't work," Holly said. "They kill chickens and bunnies, and—"

"Bats," Kate said. "Everyone loves bats."

"Not." Holly whipped out her iPhone. Seconds later she said, "Okay, how about the little brown bat, *myotis lucifugus*?"

"Sounds like the devil."

"That's *lucifer*, you idiot."

"So let's go back to the whippoorwills," Kate said. "They're cute, they're brown, and—"

"—hardly anyone knows what they are," Holly finished.

"Okay," Kate said, "I'll ask my dad."

"He's in Austria, remember?"

"Oh, right." Kate thought for a moment. "I could ask Dr. Zimmerman."

"Who's he?"

"Dad's old professor," Kate said. He'd know exactly what species were endangered and how to go about getting publicity. But when she punched in Dr. Zimmerman's number, she got voice mail that said he was out of the country and wouldn't be back until September.

Holly frowned. "Now what?"

"Aunt Bea," Kate said as they walked home across the back field. The pool looked so inviting, Kate wanted to jump in, clothes and all.

"She said not to disturb her."

"We'll pretend George Clooney called."

Laughing, they trooped into the kitchen and found Aunt Bea whipping up a Caesar salad.

"Audubon," she said after Holly explained what was going on. "That's who you want."

"But he died ages ago," Kate said.

"In eighteen fifty-one, to be precise," said Aunt Bea. "Do your research. Use the Internet, the local paper. Call the Winfield Birders' Club." Holding up a wedge of lettuce smothered in dressing and Parmesan cheese, she offered it to Holly. "Taste."

"Not enough garlic."

With a wicked grin, Aunt Bea added more.

* * *

After dinner, Kate got online while Holly scoured the *Winfield Gazette*. Adam interrupted with texts every two minutes so she didn't get very far. He would be coming to Timber Ridge this weekend with Domino, his half-

Arabian pinto, and hoped they could all go trail riding. He even offered to help with the camp kids.

"Great," Kate said. "He can take Nadine and Gabrielle."

"They'll love it," Holly said stretching out on her bed. "Adam's so cute, they'll be all over him."

"No way," Kate said. "They're not even twelve."

"So?" Holly retorted. "I had a boyfriend when I was nine."

"You did not."

"His name was Arthur and—"

"—he had four legs and a tail," Kate finished.

Holly gave an exasperated sigh. Kate didn't get it about boys, she just didn't. She'd messed up with Nathan and now Brad had dumped her.

Well, not exactly dumped, but close enough.

What she needed was "boy lessons"—how to talk to them, even flirt a little. Holly bit back a smile. She could no more imagine Kate flirting than she could imagine Angela telling the truth or Mrs. Dean volunteering at a soup kitchen.

"This might work," Kate said.

"What?"

"A petition. We'll do it online and—"

"No, it's got to be local," Holly said, hugging her favorite stuffed pony. A dozen more hung in a rope hammock above her bed. On the ceiling galloped a herd of

mustangs. Mom had put them up there after the car accident that had killed Holly's father and left Holly stuck in
bed all day with nothing to do. She knew those wild horses
like she knew the back of her hand. The leader was all
black, just like Magician.

"You mean going door-to-door?" Kate said. "At
Timber Ridge?"

"Yes," Holly said, warming to the idea. "We could
ride our horses. That always gets people's attention."

"Like at Halloween?"

"Oh, I forgot about that," Holly said.

They'd gone trick-or-treating on horseback, but instead of asking for candy they'd collected money for a
local horse rescue center. The next day Mrs. Dean accused
Kate of trampling all over her garden and threatened to
sue Kate's father. Later they found out that Angela had
done the damage, just to get Kate in trouble.

"There's got to be something else we can do," Kate said.

Holly kissed her pony, then reached for another. The
hammock came loose and all the stuffed toys landed on
top of her. "Put it on the list," she said, fending off an av-
alanche of ponies. "Right beside the *something* we've got
to do about Angela."

"We could combine them both."

"How?"

"I dunno," Kate said. "You're always the one with
bright ideas, not me."

Holly sighed and stared at her ceiling—bays, browns, and pintos galloping through sagebrush and tumbleweed, and—

She sat up so fast, her head spun. "Weed killer."

"To spray Angela with?"

"No, silly. I bet Mrs. Dean will have the builders use something illegal and poisonous to clear the ground for her stupid slide. That trail is stuffed with vines and pricker bushes and—"

"—milkweed," Kate said.

"Okay, that, too."

"No, really," Kate said. "It's important. Monarch butterflies can't survive without milkweed. It's the only plant their caterpillars eat."

"Are they in trouble?"

"Seriously. You should hear Dad go on about it. If we don't do something, we're gonna lose them."

While Kate got busy researching toxic chemicals on the web, Holly hugged her stuffed ponies and began to have doubts. How could a couple of horse-crazy girls take on the Queen of Timber Ridge . . . and win? They needed something more newsworthy than endangered birds, rare bats, and hungry caterpillars. But what?

* * *

To Kate's surprise, the horses were already munching hay when she and Holly reached the barn at six thirty the next morning. Somebody had beaten them to it, but it couldn't be Mrs. Dean's new trainer. She hadn't shown up until ten o'clock yesterday.

"Who's there?" Holly called out.

Dragging a trunk with her saddle and bridle perched on top, Sue emerged from the tack room. She looked up, eyes wide with surprise—or maybe guilt—as if she hadn't expected to see anyone at the barn so early. "Oh, I didn't—"

Immediately, Kate was taken back to that cold lonely night in February when she'd snuck into the barn to retrieve her own saddle and bridle—right after Mrs. Dean had thrown her out. This wasn't the same, but Kate knew how Sue felt—isolated and miserable. Her eyes were red, her freckled face blotchy with tears.

"Did you feed?" Holly said.

"No, just hay." Sue refused to meet Kate's eyes. "To keep them quiet while—"

"—you left without saying good-bye?"

A tear trickled down Sue's cheeks. "I couldn't face it. I'm sorry."

She looked so unhappy that all of Kate's resentment drained away. Sue had been a good friend. From the beginning, she'd made Kate welcome at Timber Ridge and she'd made her laugh when Angela was being impossible.

Just then, Ragtime interrupted with a bellowing neigh, followed by Kristina's palomino, Cody, who banged a rapid tattoo on his door. This set all the others off, and in seconds the barn was in an uproar. Even Tapestry paced her stall. Hay was no longer good enough. The horses wanted their grain.

Like, right *now*.

"Okay, okay," Holly yelled. "Don't get your knickers in a knot."

It broke the tension. Sue gave a weak smile, and Holly said they'd better hustle or they'd have a mutiny on their hands. She uncoiled the hose and began to fill water buckets.

"I really am sorry," Sue said as she helped Kate measure out the grain. "About Brad, and everything."

Kate didn't know what to say. She got embarrassed when people apologized and she always ended up feeling guilty, as if she'd done something wrong or had hurt someone's feelings by mistake.

She shrugged. "It's all right."

"I don't want to move," Sue said. "I really don't."

Kate hesitated. "How does Brad feel about it?"

"My brother will be in snowboarding heaven," Sue said. "And the high school wants him on their varsity football team." With a sigh, she slumped against the grain bin. "Dad's saying it'll be a whole new adventure and Mom's telling me to make the best of it and that I'll make new friends. But I won't. My friends are all here. I don't know anyone out there."

"You'll be fine," Kate said. "You'll find a crowd of horse girls, and—"

"—they'll tease me for riding English."

"Then you'll have to tease them right back," Kate said dishing out advice she wished she could follow herself. "And then you'll have to show them how good you are." She added supplements to the horses' breakfast. "Maybe you'll learn to ride Western."

"Yeah," Sue said. "I'll become a rodeo queen."

"No, really," Kate said. "I've seen those girls ride and it looks like they're having fun. They even have Western dressage."

"They do?" Sue said.

"Check it out."

Magician banged on his door, so Kate grabbed her buckets. Last fall, this had almost happened to her. If Dad hadn't given up his academic career and bought the butterfly museum, he and Kate would be living in Wyoming— over two thousand miles away. She knew how Sue felt.

More or less.

"What about Tara?" Holly said as she dragged her hose over to the Appaloosa's stall. "Is she going with you?"

Sue's eyes filled with tears again. "We can't afford it. Dad says I can get another horse out there, but not right away."

"Oh, no," Holly said. "That's awful."

This was something else Kate understood. When her father was planning their move last fall, he told Kate it wasn't worth shipping Tapestry to Wyoming because they had plenty of horses out west. She'd been totally devastated and had refused to go. Luckily, she didn't have to.

"I'm sorry," Kate said. "Let's go out for pizza tonight."

"And ice cream," Holly said. "I'll get Aunt Bea to drive us."

"I can't," Sue said. "We're leaving at four in the morning, and I've still got a ton of packing to do. Mom wants everyone in bed by eight."

So they said goodbye in the barn. Amid sniffs and tears, they hugged one another. They promised to text and post on each other's Facebook pages, and then they hugged Tara. She'd already been sold to a guy in New Hampshire who'd be coming to collect her the next day.

"He rides Western," Sue said.

"And I bet Tara will be fantastic at it," Kate said.

Sue gave Kate an ironic grin. "Funny how things work out, isn't it."

8

AT NINE, THE CAMP KIDS ARRIVED with sticky fingers and smelling of maple syrup. "We had waffles for breakfast," Charlotte said.

"With strawberries," added Laura.

Gently, Kate wiped a blob of whipped cream off Marcia's chin. "Are you guys ready to work?"

"Yes," Eden whispered.

She'd appeared out of nowhere. For a moment, her pale blue eyes and wispy brown hair didn't register. Kate couldn't even remember the pony she'd ridden. Oh, yes, the roan. Kate racked her brains for its name.

"Jester?" she said.

Eden blushed. "Jinx."

The barn door slid open, and Angela's mother tottered inside wearing the most ridiculous boots Kate had ever seen. Tight and shiny with three-inch heels, they looked as if they'd been painted onto Mrs. Dean's skinny legs.

"Listen up, girls," she said. "We have a small change of plans."

Behind her, Angela and Kristina nudged one another. So, what was going on now? Kate shot a look at Holly. The last thing they needed was another of Mrs. Dean's changes. An hour ago, two bulldozers had rumbled past the barn, and Holly had asked one of the drivers where they were going.

"To dig a foundation for the slide."

It didn't make any sense. Why would Mrs. Dean have gone to the expense of fixing up the jumps only to build a carnival ride in the next field? There were other slopes on the mountain where an alpine slide would work, but there weren't any other meadows big enough and flat enough for a hunt course.

"What sort of change?" Kate said.

She was probably getting herself into even more trouble, challenging Angela's mother like this, but Kate didn't care. Somebody had to ask the tough questions, and it might as well be her.

Mrs. Dean sniffed. "Jocelyn Fraser won't be with us any more."

"She wasn't with us in the first place," Holly said.

A couple of the little kids sniggered.

There was a pause, then Mrs. Dean said, "I hope to arrange for some clinics next week, but in the meantime you older girls will take over."

"Us?" Kate said.

Ignoring her, Mrs. Dean went on. "You will each mentor two girls, in teams of four. Angela will have Laura and Charlotte, and Kristina will take Amber and Gabrielle."

With one stroke, Mrs. Dean had picked the four richest kids for Angela's team. And this was fine, as far as Kate was concerned, but she seriously doubted that Angela and Kristina would actually pitch in with barn chores and teach the rich kids how to take care of their own ponies. Wasn't that what horse camp was all about?

As for the clinics, Mrs. Dean was off-the-wall crazy. She'd never find anyone at the last minute, especially for a minor barn in the middle of Vermont.

"No," Kate said.

Mrs. Dean glared at her. "Excuse me?"

For a wild-and-crazy moment the barn stood still. Even the horses stopped rattling their buckets. Kate took a deep breath and something inside her snapped. She counted to three—no sense in going off like a loose cannon—and looked Mrs. Dean straight in the eye.

"No," Kate said again. "If you want us to help, then tell Angela and Kristina to help as well. So far they've done nothing."

"*Liar*," Angela said.

Holly rounded on her. "Oh, yeah? All you do is lounge about in your fancy white breeches and complain if they get dirty. You never muck stalls or groom your horse, and I don't think I've ever seen you clean tack."

Angela shifted sideways, but Holly went with her. It almost looked as if she were going to prod Angela's chest the way she'd prodded Prince Ferdinand's in England.

"So, tell me," Holly spat out, her nose inches away from Angela's. "What's the last useful thing you and Kristina did around here?"

"Oh, we—" Kristina said.

Angela folded her arms. "I don't need to prove myself."

"That's because you can't," Kate said.

There was a shocked silence. Kate could feel it smothering her as the wide-eyed camp kids shuffled their feet, watching her and Holly take on Mrs. Dean and wondering who would win.

Kate's self-confidence faltered. If she kept pushing Mrs. Dean, she could find herself banned from the barn. Even worse, Liz could find herself out of a job.

Mrs. Dean made a noise in her throat like a dog about to throw up. She took a step backward, but her heel caught on a clump of manure and it was only Angela's quick reaction that saved her mother from toppling right over. From the corner of her eye, Kate saw Holly punching the air with her fist.

Score one for us!

But Mrs. Dean recovered fast. "I'm sure you girls will work it out," she said in icy tones. "Now hurry up. We haven't got all day."

* * *

The moment Mrs. Dean stalked off, Holly announced a time-out. This whole thing was a fiasco, and if she and Kate didn't do something, it would reflect badly on Mom. Her contract to run the barn was supposed to be good for another year, but Holly didn't trust Mrs. Dean any further than she could throw her.

It was time to get serious.

With a quick look at Kate, Holly shunted their four campers into the tack room and told them to wipe off their saddles and wash their horses' bits. Marcia got busy right away, showing Eden how to take a bridle apart.

Nadine scowled. "I don't do this at home."

"Neither do I," said Maeve. "We have grooms."

"You're not at home now," Holly snapped, "so get on with it. We'll be back in ten minutes." Then she nodded at Kate. "Come on."

"Where to?"

"The indoor," Holly said, slamming the tack room door so hard its hinges rattled.

"Why?" Kate said.

"Strategy meeting." Holly grabbed Kate's hand and

dragged her down the aisle and into the indoor arena. One of the boarders was schooling her gray Thoroughbred at the far end.

"What about her?" Kate said.

"She won't bother with us," Holly said as they slipped into the observation booth. She closed that door as well, then flipped open a folding chair and straddled it backward, facing Kate. "This camp gig is not what we signed up for."

"I don't remember signing up for anything," Kate said looking mutinous. "Mrs. Dean has tricked us into it."

"We can't refuse."

"Well, we *could*," Kate said, "but—

"—if we do," Holly interrupted before Kate could go any further, "it'll be bad for Mom."

Kate sighed. "I know."

"So you'll do it?"

"Of course, I will," Kate said.

Holly let out her breath. "Thanks."

"Okay," Kate said. "But suppose, just for a minute, that we don't go along with Mrs. Dean. What then?"

"The camp will fall apart and Mrs. Dean will blame Mom, never mind that she's not here and it wasn't her idea in the first place."

Kate sighed. "I was afraid of that."

"So, the way I see it," Holly said, "is that we've got two choices. We can goof off, which is what Angela and

Kristina will be doing, or we can give these kids the best camp they've ever had." She looked at Kate. "But there's only one problem. Two, actually."

"What?"

"I've never been to camp. Have you?"

"No."

"Then we'll have to make it up as we go along," Holly said. "It can't be that hard, but—"

"What's the other problem?" Kate said.

"Charlotte. She won't last five minutes with Angela."

"And Angela won't last five minutes with Charlotte's horse," Kate said. "You heard what she called Elke."

"A dump truck."

"So let's offer Angela a swap. She can have one of our kids and we'll take Charlotte."

"Okay, and while we're at it, let's try and rescue Laura as well," Holly said.

"How?"

"Easy. We just wait till Angela gets fed up with them. It won't take long."

"So who do we give up?" Kate said.

"Let Angela choose. That way we can't be accused of favoritism."

Slowly, Kate nodded. "She won't pick her stepsister."

"Or Eden," Holly said.

"Why not?"

"Because Angela doesn't like roans any more than she

likes Fjords," Holly said. "They don't fit with her color
scheme. Plus Eden's too quiet. Angela probably hasn't
even noticed she's around."

"So, how long should we wait?"

"I reckon half an hour should do it." Holly bent to
scoop a curb chain off the floor. It was probably the one
that Angela had accused Kate of stealing a couple of days
ago, which was ridiculous because Kate didn't use a curb
bit.

None of them did, except Angela.

The gray Thoroughbred let out a piercing whinny.
Ears pricked, he danced about, almost unseating his rider.
Another horse answered, so Holly yanked open the
booth's door.

At first, she couldn't see properly because the light was
wrong. But then, through the gloom, came Charlotte and
Laura—faces grim with determination—leading their
ponies toward her.

"Whoops," Holly said. "It only took ten minutes."

"What did?" Kate said.

"The girls." Holly grinned. "They've jumped ship."

* * *

Angela met them outside the tack room. "*Your* campers
have locked me out."

"Sorry," Kate said. "Open up, girls."

The handle rattled and finally the door swung open. It

must've locked by itself when Holly slammed it. Marcia looked at her former stepsister with hugely innocent brown eyes.

She said, "We didn't know it was—"

"Yes, you did." Angela shoved past her.

In a flash, Nadine and Maeve attached themselves to Angela like a pair of barnacles. Whatever they'd been trying to clean landed on the floor. A twisted wire snaffle bounced off Robin's tack trunk. Kate picked it up.

Twisted?

"Who owns this?" she said.

"Me," Nadine said and snatched it back.

Kate was about to suggest a milder bit for Nadine's pony when she remembered that Angela would be taking over—if she agreed to trading kids. But it looked as if she already had, because without missing a beat she turned and swept out the door with Maeve and Nadine skipping after her like obedient puppies.

"Well, that was easy," Holly said.

"Too easy," Kate said, wondering if Angela had somehow planned it all along.

9

WHILE MARCIA AND LAURA GROOMED their horses, Kate helped Charlotte. The little girl had no idea how to pick out Elke's feet or even that it needed to be done. And when Kate showed her the underside of Elke's hoof, Charlotte acted as if she'd never seen anything like it before.

She pointed. "What's that?"

"The frog," Kate said. "And—"

"*Frog?*" Charlotte said. "Why is it called a frog?"

"Because it kind of looks like one," Kate said. There were other reasons for the odd name, based on myth and Scottish folktales, but those stories were best saved for nights around a campfire with toasted marshmallows and a sing-along. Not that Mrs. Dean would allow it. She'd already made that quite clear. Her precious kids weren't going to sleep in tents.

Gently, Charlotte poked Elke's frog. "It's squishy, like a real one."

"So," Kate teased, "how many other frogs have you poked lately?"

"You don't poke frogs," Charlotte said rolling her eyes as if Kate was too stupid to live. "You *kiss* them, and then you get a prince." She gave Kate a shy smile. "Or a cute guy."

"Okay, got it," Kate said.

Except, for her, it had worked in reverse. The last two cute guys she'd kissed had turned into very large frogs. She finished scraping dirt from Elke's hoof, then showed Charlotte how to pick out the others. Obediently, Elke lifted each leg and didn't even flinch when Charlotte's hoof pick slipped and scraped into her tender pastern by mistake.

Next came grooming and Charlotte wasn't much good at that, either. She didn't know what to do with a curry comb and couldn't get her small hands around a body brush. Even brushing Elke's tail turned into a struggle.

"Haven't you done this before?" Kate said.

"I wasn't allowed to."

"Why not?"

"My trainer said I got in the way and that I should work on my riding because that's what my mom was paying for."

Kate sighed.

It was the same at her old barn in Connecticut. The

rich kids showed up to ride their expensive warmbloods and left the dirty work to girls like Kate, who groomed, cleaned tack, and mucked stalls in return for riding lessons.

"What about the others?" she said. "Nadine and Maeve and—"

"They don't know how to groom either, and they don't care."

"But you do?"

"Yes." Charlotte's voice was so soft, Kate barely heard it. "But I don't want to jump."

"No problem," Kate said. "You don't have to do anything that makes you uncomfortable. Now, take Elke into the aisle and put her on the crossties. I'll help you put her saddle on."

This was the easy part, teaching kids how to groom and tack up their horses. Giving riding lessons was a whole other ball game, and Kate was a bit apprehensive.

Suppose one of the kids fell off and got hurt or an angry mother bawled them out for teaching her pony-hunter daughter a little dressage. There was a big divide between the two disciplines. Kate had seen it in action at her old barn. The big eq riders looked down their noses at the girls who competed in three-day events. It went the other way as well.

Ridiculous, Kate thought.

They all loved horses, so why couldn't everyone just

get along and learn from one another instead of dissing each other's riding style? On her way out of the barn, Kate grabbed a cavesson, whip, and lunge line and then shared her concerns with Holly as they followed their students to the outdoor ring.

"Relax," Holly said. "The kids are here to have fun, not become the next Olympic champions."

"I just want them to survive."

"And they will." Holly opened the gate and stood back to let the kids inside. "But if you're really determined to worry, then worry about the other four kids who're stuck with Angela and Kristina."

* * *

For the first half hour, they split the girls up. Holly took Laura, Marcia, and Eden, while Kate worked with Charlotte on the lunge line. It hadn't rained in over a week, and the ring was dry and dusty. It was also hot. Kate thought longingly of the pool at Holly's house. No, not *Holly's* house. It was now hers as well—and Dad's. Well, it would be once he and Liz bought it.

"Trot on," Kate said to Charlotte.

She wasn't doing too badly now that she'd learned to relax her hands and put her feet in the stirrups correctly. Elke was a saint. No matter what Charlotte did, the mare soldiered on. At one point, an empty plastic bag drifted across the ring, and Elke didn't even falter. She just kept trotting. Tapestry would've had a bird. So would Magician.

Plastic monsters? Big teeth! Oh, no!

But nothing seemed to faze the unflappable Fjord. She'd blow everyone else out of the water in a trail class.

Trail?

Why not? Kate added it to her list of suggestions for Mrs. Dean. She'd called a five o'clock meeting in Liz's office at the barn. They would be discussing Saturday's scavenger hunt and the end-of-camp show.

* * *

"A *trail* class?" Holly said when Kate mentioned her plans. They'd run home for lunch and were about to cool off in the pool before heading back to the barn.

Kate frowned. "Why not?"

"It's a Western event."

"So?"

"This morning you were worried about getting in trouble for teaching a little dressage," Holly said, dropping her ratty old Scooby Doo towel onto a chaise. "A trail class would be ten times worse."

Kate hadn't thought of that. "Yes, but—"

"C'mon, I'll race you," Holly said. She walked to the deep end, flexing her arms. "Four laps, and the loser gets to tell Mrs. Dean we're having a gymkhana."

"Not fair," Kate said. "You always win."

Holly grinned. "So try harder."

On the count of three, they dived in, but no matter how hard Kate tried, she couldn't keep up with Holly. At the end of two laps, she was half a length behind. By the time she made the final turn, her brand-new sister was already climbing out of the pool. With a laugh, Holly shook her long hair and droplets of water flew out.

In her shimmering blue tankini, Holly reminded Kate of a mermaid. She swam like one, too, thanks to hundreds of hours in the pool. Swimming had been Holly's only exercise when she was stuck in her wheelchair for two years, and she was seriously good at it. None of the boys in their class could beat her—not even in the butterfly—and the swimming coach wanted her on the high school team, but Holly refused. Swim practice took time away from riding.

"What's on for this afternoon?" Kate said.

"Mrs. Dean's meeting, remember?"

"No, before that," Kate said toweling off her hair. "What shall we do with the kids?"

"My three want to jump."

"Charlotte won't."

"So set up something she *will* do," Holly said. "Like a—"

"—trail course?"

"That'd work. Just don't let Angela see you teaching Charlotte how to deal with the obstacles."

"That's *it*," Kate cried. "You're a genius."

"I am?"

"We'll call it an obstacle course, not a trail class," Kate said. "Mrs. Dean won't know the difference anyway."

* * *

Charlotte and Elke took to Kate's obstacle course like a pony to apples and carrots. The mare didn't bat an eyelash when Kate led her over a blue tarp, and she didn't even hesitate when confronted with a circle of old tires. She just gave a little snort as if to say, "What's the big deal?" and then stepped inside each tire as carefully as if she were treading on eggshells.

Opening gates was a walk in the park.

So were trotting over poles on the ground and bending around traffic cones. The only glitch came when Charlotte asked her horse to back up between two long window boxes filled with plastic flowers. Elke wanted to eat them.

"Looking good," Holly said.

"Thanks, but I need more ideas for obstacles," Kate said as she watched Charlotte negotiate the flower boxes again. This time, Elke didn't try for a snack. "Five isn't enough."

"Then ask Mr. Evans," Holly said. "He rides Western, and Aunt Bea said he's coming for dinner tonight."

"Cool," Kate said.

She liked Mr. Evans. He'd given her a stall for Tapestry in February after Mrs. Dean had thrown them out of

Timber Ridge. His tiny barn was so neat and clean, you could actually live in it. But it was lonely. No other kids—just Max, the barn's inscrutable red tabby, and Mr. Evans's horse, Pardner, which he'd bought at the same auction where Kate had found Tapestry.

After Charlotte got through with the trail course and Holly's campers finished their last jump-off, they called it quits and headed for the barn—except they couldn't get inside. Muck buckets blocked the doorway, pitchforks lay strewn on the ground, and a broken rake leaned against two open bales of hay that spilled into the aisle.

"Hey, wait a minute," Kate said. "Who left this mess?" She raised her voice. "Angela?"

No answer.

"Dream on," Holly said. "She's probably at the club."

With an angry sigh, Kate shoved a muck bucket out of her way. It toppled over and clumps of manure tumbled across the aisle, now littered with candy wrappers and crumpled soda cans. If Liz ever saw this, she'd flip out.

"I'll clean it up," Marcia said.

Kate rounded on her. "No, you won't."

"Why not?"

"Because it's Angela's job," Kate said. "And her campers. They made this mess, and they can take care of it."

* * *

At the last minute, Mrs. Dean switched gears and held the meeting at her house instead of in Liz's office. "It's too hot in the barn," she said, leading the girls into her living room. An oil painting of Angela wearing a shadbelly, a yellow vest, and a top hat hung above the oak mantel.

"It's also too messy," Kate said, trying not to stare at the portrait. It was beyond ridiculous. She even felt sorry for Angela, who didn't look too happy at being trussed up in riding clothes she had no business wearing.

Mrs. Dean raised a well-plucked eyebrow. "Oh?"

"Yeah," Holly said. "Angela and Kristina trashed it."

The air conditioning was cranked up so high that goosebumps erupted on Kate's arms. Was she nervous or just freezing cold? Nerves, probably. She felt Holly squeeze her hand.

You can do it.

"But that's not all," Kate said, forcing herself to look at Mrs. Dean. "This morning, Holly and I fed the horses, mucked twenty stalls, and raked the aisle—by ourselves. Angela and Kristina never showed up."

"They were helping me," Mrs. Dean said.

"At six thirty?"

"Yes," Angela said. "Mother needed—"

"—help with getting dressed?"

Beside her, Kate heard Holly's breath come out in a whoosh. Oh boy, she'd be in trouble now. But to her relief,

Mrs. Dean carried on as if Kate hadn't even spoken. "So, Angela, what have you and Kristina decided for the horse show?"

"Equitation, jumping, and—"

"—a gymkhana," Kate finished.

Angela looked at her as if she'd gone completely mad. "*Gymkhana?* That's Western stuff," she spat out. "We don't do that here."

"*Gymkhana* is an Indian word, and—"

"Indians?" said Mrs. Dean. "What have those illiterate fools got to do with it? They're an absolute nuisance—always complaining about us building houses and shopping centers and how we're desecrating their tribal lands."

"Not Native Americans," Kate said, barely able to conceal her disgust. "India, the country."

A dreamy expression softened Mrs. Dean's face. For a second or two, she looked almost normal. "My great-great grandfather served in India," she said. "He was a colonel in the British army and a very talented rider." Leaning across the coffee table, she patted her daughter's knee. "As you can tell, it runs in our family."

"The word *gymkhana*," Kate said, 'means mounted games.'" It didn't really, but according to her hurried research it was close enough, and "mounted games" sounded even better than an "obstacle course."

Mrs. Dean looked dubious.

"The cavalry officers used to play games on horseback to keep themselves fit and ready for battle," Kate went on, hoping that Mrs. Dean would take the bait. "The Pony Club in England has been playing mounted games, like, forever at big shows in London."

"Really?"

"And they're sponsored by Prince Philip."

"Oh, that's perfect, just perfect," said Mrs. Dean.

Holly nudged Kate; Kate nudged her back. This was exactly what they'd been hoping for—Mrs. Dean, getting all excited about royal connections, even if it was totally ridiculous.

A dozen gold bracelets jangled as Mrs. Dean clapped her hands. "Now, Angela, you must add mounted games to our list. They will go down very well with our audience." She flashed a rare smile. "And be sure to tell everyone they are *royal* games."

Kate masked her sigh with a cough. She caught Holly's eye and almost burst out laughing. Fooling Mrs. Dean was so easy, it was like taking candy from a baby.

"Yes, *mother*." Angela glared at Kate and tapped her iPad so hard it almost bounced off her lap.

"Can we talk about the scavenger hunt?" Holly said. "We need to figure out what sort of things the kids need to look for."

Kristina yawned. "Must we?"

"Yes." Mrs. Dean stood up. "You girls go ahead. I have a call to make."

* * *

An hour later, Kate and Holly checked the barn. Someone had cleaned it up. That phone call Mrs. Dean made while they were arguing about the scavenger hunt had obviously been to the maintenance crew. One of their green trucks had driven past as they left the Deans' house.

"You're all set, now," the driver had yelled.

10

THEY WERE TUCKING INTO DESSERT when Aunt Bea said, "I've been snooping."

"So, what else is new?" Kate said with a grin.

Holly's aunt was a cross between Harriet the Spy and Ms. Frizzle from *The Magic School Bus*. She was always on the lookout for clues and things that didn't quite add up.

Like Mrs. Dean's latest scheme?

Holly helped herself to another slice of blueberry pie and waved her fork at Aunt Bea. "Don't mind Kate. She's had a bad day."

"Let me guess," said Aunt Bea. "Mrs. Dean?"

"How did you know?"

Aunt Bea took a sip of coffee. "Because I went to the town hall this morning and poked through the public tax records. It seems that Mrs. Dean has a lot of money tied up in property development. In the last three months she's bought seven empty houses at Timber Ridge."

Mr. Evans whistled. "That's impressive."

"But, why?" Kate said.

"In the hopes of selling them for a profit," said Aunt Bea. "But also because she doesn't want the *Home for Sale* signs out there in full view. It'll look bad to potential buyers. So I'm guessing that Timber Ridge is in financial trouble and that's why she's going nuts with improvements."

"To attract the rich and famous?" Holly said.

"Yep."

"In that case," said Mr. Evans, "an alpine slide won't cut it. She needs a world-class golf course, a celebrity tennis coach, or—"

"—a big name horse trainer?" Kate said.

Aunt Bea nodded. "Let's hope it doesn't come to that. Now tell me about camp. What have you decided for the show? Do you need any help?"

"Yes," Kate said suddenly remembering that she needed to ask Mr. Evans about trail classes. In less than two minutes he tossed out several great suggestions, then offered to judge the class.

"Wow, thanks," Kate said. "That would be awesome."

"But don't wear your cowboy boots," warned Aunt

Bea, "or your Stetson. This is an English crowd, remember?"

"Got it," he said.

Holly pulled a frowny face. "You should've heard Kate bamboozling Mrs. Dean about gymkhanas," she said. "Kate told her that *gymkhana* was an Indian word, and Mrs. Dean got all snotty because she thought Kate was talking about Native Americans."

"She called them a nuisance," Kate said.

"*And* illiterate," Holly said.

Aunt Bea glanced at Mr. Evans. "Maybe Mrs. Dean needs to meet David Wickett."

"Who's that?" Holly said.

"An Abenaki chief and a successful attorney," said Mr. Evans. "David and I were roommates in college. He works for the governor of Vermont." He smiled at Kate. "Now, tell me again where Mrs. Dean's alpine slide is."

"On a slope beside the hunt course."

"I'd like to see it."

"Come on Saturday," Kate said. "You can watch us do the scavenger hunt."

If she and Holly managed to pull it off. Their discussion with Angela and Kristina had devolved into a dumb argument over what the kids should be wearing for the ride. Angela had insisted on the lime green camp t-shirts her mother had provided; Kate said it didn't matter as long as they wore helmets and riding boots.

"Better yet," Mr. Evans said. "I'll do it myself."

"You're too old," said Aunt Bea.

"Maybe," he said with a grin that lit up his homely face. "But that won't stop me."

* * *

To Kate's relief, Aunt Bea offered to organize the scavenger hunt. She would make a list of things the kids needed to find and then photograph. They wouldn't be bringing anything back to the barn except pictures and videos on their cell phones.

"Like what?" Holly said.

Aunt Bea touched her nose. "That's for me to know and you to find out."

On Thursday morning, the UPS guy delivered a box of ribbons that Mrs. Dean had ordered. Kate took a peek inside. Eight of every color, including orange and purple. Clearly, Mrs. Dean didn't want any of her camp kids going home without ribbons. She'd also ordered giant Hershey's kisses—gold and silver for the grand prize winners, plus a bunch of small and middle-sized ones.

Kate thawed a little.

Was this a side of Angela's mother she'd never seen or was it just a marketing ploy? Happy kids made even happier parents. Apparently, they'd all be there at the end-of-camp show, including Charlotte's mother. Kate had asked

Charlotte if her dad would come too, but Charlotte didn't know.

Or wasn't saying.

Whenever Kate asked about her family, Charlotte shut her face down like a mouse that had scurried into its hole and slammed the door behind it.

* * *

After a combined lesson with Angela's group in the outdoor ring, they all went for a trail ride. Kate had argued Angela into it.

"It's too hot," she'd whined. "Let's go swimming at the club."

But Kate insisted because she wanted to make sure the new kids could find their way around the trails that circled the base of Timber Ridge Mountain so they'd be ready for the scavenger hunt. Angela didn't seem to care. Maybe she'd have been just as happy if the kids got lost.

Sunlight filtered through the trees and dappled the horses' glossy coats. Even Elke had a shine on her dun-colored rump. It was hard to be grumpy on a day like this, even if your arms ached from mucking stalls and you wanted to yell at Angela for doing pretty much nothing.

She'd showed up at nine with Kristina, and they'd pretended to help by rearranging saddles in the tack room. All the horses had nameplates beneath their racks, so this maneuver made absolutely no sense. Then they switched them all back again. After that, they'd idled about, getting in the way and arguing with each other about what color nail polish went best with their new scarlet polo shirts.

"Do something useful," Holly had growled.

And now, from what Kate could tell, Angela and Kristina were still discussing nail polish and totally ignoring their four campers. Maeve had trotted ahead and Amber lagged so far behind, she was almost out of sight.

Kate pulled Rebel to one side.

Almost immediately, Sandcastle bolted past with Gabrielle hanging on for dear life amid a blur of flying mane and pounding hooves.

"Hold up," Kate yelled.

Too late.

Sandcastle had the bit between his teeth and wasn't about to let go. But Gabrielle did—except her foot got caught in the stirrup and she was dragged several yards before Holly and Magician blocked the pony's path.

"Whoa," Holly said grabbing Sandcastle's reins.

The runaway pony skidded to an awkward halt. Kate cantered up and jumped off Rebel. She released Gabrielle's foot from her stirrup. "Are you okay?"

"I think so."

Kate helped the little girl to stand up. She didn't seem hurt, just dazed and covered with leaves and twigs. Gently, Kate brushed them off. "Don't try to walk."

"I need to get back on," Gabrielle said. "My instructor—"

"Yes, but catch your breath first."

Ears pinned, Sandcastle lunged at Kate's arm. She jerked it away just in time and gave the troublesome gelding a gentle cuff on his nose. "Stop that."

This pony was a disaster. He may have been a showstopper in the hunter ring, but he had no business with a novice rider on his back—or anyone else for that matter, at least not until someone had taught him a few manners. And while they were at it, maybe they could teach Angela, too. She and Kristina had ridden off, leaving Kate and Holly to cope with all the campers.

Kate gave Gabrielle a leg-up. "Sure you're okay?"

"Yes." Gabrielle smiled.

She looked surprisingly cheerful for a kid who'd just been dragged by her pony, now happily cropping grass. Even so, Kate didn't trust Sandcastle, and she kept a watchful eye on them both as they rode onto the hunt course. Piles of dirt loomed beyond the far hedge, but the earth-moving equipment was silent. No sign of any workmen, either. Lunch break, maybe?

Holly said, "Go and check it out."

"Why?"

"Because we need to know what's going on," Holly said. "I'll watch out for the kids."

"Okay."

There was a gap in the hedge. Ducking a low-hanging branch, Kate urged Rebel along the narrow path. Brambles tore at her legs and burrs clung to Rebel's mane. She'd have a fine old time pulling them out. His mane was even longer than Tapestry's.

On the other side of the hedge, Kate gasped.

The entire slope was a moonscape, arid and bare like something from a science fiction movie. No undergrowth, no grass or wildflowers—just a deep trench that snaked its ugly way up the trail between piles of dirt and rubble. Inside it were parallel tracks—grooved metal tubes with supports every ten feet or so like a LEGO set gone completely mad.

For a few moments, Kate just sat there. She could almost hear kids shrieking as they zoomed down the hill on those rattling carts, scared out of their wits but loving it. At the bottom would be hot-dog stands, cotton candy stalls, shops selling tacky souvenirs, and crowds lining up for their turn on the slide. It might even be lots of fun . . .

If only it wasn't here.

* * *

On Saturday morning Aunt Bea pulled a surprise. She gathered the kids and their counselors at ten o'clock and announced that the leaders had to swap.

"Like, swap teams?" Holly said.

Angela tossed her head. "No way."

"It's only fair," said Aunt Bea.

"That's dumb," Angela retorted. "I want to win."

"And that's why you'll be leading the other team."

It took a moment for it all to sink in, and Kate had to bite her lip to keep from laughing out loud as she watched Angela's horrified expression.

Aunt Bea went on. "These kids don't know the mountain, and you do. So it's up to you to keep them safe and show them a good time. This isn't a grand prix, it's a scavenger hunt. Take pictures of the stuff on my list, ask questions, and learn a few things about nature." She checked her notes. "The teams will be scored on how well they do and also on how their leaders help them. So get out there and do your best."

"What about me?" Holly said. "And Adam?"

He'd just arrived with Domino. Kate grinned at him, knowing how much of a swivet Holly had been in, checking her watch and worrying that he wouldn't show up in time for the scavenger hunt.

"You guys will hold the fort," said Aunt Bea. "And so will Kristina. When everyone gets back, there'll be a barbecue and all the ice cream you can eat."

"Buttercrunch?" Holly said sounding hopeful.

"A bucket load," said Aunt Bea.

Her special friend, Earl Evans, wheeled his horse around. He couldn't compete like he wanted to because he'd helped Aunt Bea set the course and write the clues.

They'd been out on the mountain most of Friday, riding the trails together and coming up with obscure clues that Kate was sure would have them all baffled, just like in Aunt Bea's mystery books.

Nobody had seen the clues, not even Mrs. Dean, but she didn't seem to give a hoot. She was relieved, so Holly maintained, that she didn't have to organize the scavenger hunt by herself. It was a whole lot more complicated than anyone had imagined. First off, the camp kids didn't know the mountain. Second of all—

Aunt Bea's whistle blew and they were off.

Earl and Pardner led the way to the first fork where the two teams would separate, then he wheeled off and promised to keep in touch via cell phone.

"Call if you need help," he said.

Kate nodded. "Thanks."

Not that it would do much good. Cell service on the mountain was notoriously bad.

Kate led Angela's team into the woods. The plan was for both teams to gather clues in opposite directions. While Angela's team was figuring out clue number one, Kate's team would be solving number ten. They would pass in the middle, somewhere between clues five and six, providing that both teams had solved the other clues correctly.

As Angela and her kids disappeared, Kate heaved a sigh of relief. At the last minute Marcia had decided not to ride Tapestry and to take Daisy instead. This had required a fast grooming because Daisy was none too clean. But Marcia didn't care. While saddling up the pinto, she'd shot a look at Kate that said, *No way am I riding your horse with my stepsister in charge.*

"Thanks," Kate had said.

And now, she dropped her hands on each side of Tapestry's wonderfully familiar withers and stretched them far apart. The mare wiggled her ears as if to say she was waiting for the next signal and would Kate please hurry up because there were trails to ride and fences to jump and could they just get on with it?

Kate signaled Angela's team to follow her.

11

THEY RODE IN A COMFORTABLE SILENCE, their horses' hoofbeats punctuated now and then by snapping twigs, rustling leaves, and birds chirping overhead. Gently, Kate scratched Tapestry's withers, then ran through the names of Angela's camp kids—Nadine, Maeve, Amber, and Gabrielle with the difficult Sandcastle. If Kate's luck held out, that pony would behave himself. So far, he was trotting along in last place, minding his own business.

After much argument with her teammates, Maeve solved their first clue—number ten on Aunt Bea's list—and aimed her cell phone at a pinecone shaped like a banana.

"Yes," she shouted, waving her phone with glee as if she'd just photographed the Loch Ness Monster.

"Great," Kate said. "Who'll get the next one?"

"Me," Amber said.

Kate slapped her a high five, and the girl actually smiled. But her smile dimmed a hundred yards further on when Nadine spotted a funny shaped rock covered in moss. It had googly eyes, just like a frog.

"This one," Nadine yelled and snapped off a picture.

Kate checked her list. Sure enough, it qualified. Aunt Bea had told the kids to watch out for Kermit's older—and much uglier—brother, and Kate wondered if Charlotte would have a giggle over this when her team got here. In a few more clues both teams would meet halfway, but only if both leaders kept their girls on track.

Counting backward, clues eight and seven involved the girls photographing odd-looking driftwood and their ponies paddling in shallow water. They took care of both on the beach at Crescent Lake, and then doubled back toward the hunt course. Clue number six told them to look for a yellow dinosaur.

"A dinosaur?" Maeve said, wide-eyed.

Gabrielle jerked Sandcastle to a halt. "Not a real one, stupid."

The pony tossed his head, and Kate winced. No wonder he was such a beast with a rider who didn't respect his mouth.

"Mind your hands," she warned. "How would you feel if someone did that to you?"

"He doesn't care."

"Yes, he does," Kate said.

Gabrielle scowled. "He's got a mouth like iron."

"That's because—" Kate started and checked herself. This wasn't the time or place for a lecture about soft hands and why they were so important. When they got back to the barn she'd have a quiet word with Gabrielle, providing Angela didn't get in their faces and start an argument. And, even if she did, Kate would overrule her—she hoped.

Ten minutes later they reached the hunt course, and Kate glanced at the hedge on its far side. The bulldozers and bucket loaders were silent, probably because it was Saturday and the construction crew was taking a day off, never mind if Mrs. Dean had demanded overtime.

All Kate could see were mounds of orange dirt studded with shovels and pickaxes—an ugly sore on the mountain. Adding to the dystopian landscape were the claws of two yellow backhoes that reared their monstrous heads above the hedge.

"Dinosaurs?" Maeve said.

Gabrielle snorted. "Told you."

Wheeling Sandcastle around, she aimed her pony at the nearest jump. He refused and Gabrielle landed halfway up his neck. Kate was about to bawl her out, when she heard shouting—from the other side of the hedge.

"Hold up," she called to the kids.

Nadine pulled a face. "Why?"

"Because I said so."

Waving at the girls to stay behind her, Kate rode toward the hedge. She pushed Tapestry between prickers and brambles and emerged on the other side in time to see Ragtime bumping into Marcia's horse so hard that Daisy dropped a shoulder and Marcia lurched forward.

"No!" Kate yelled, but too late.

It all seemed to happen in slow motion. Marcia tumbled off her horse and disappeared. Into the trench she fell. It wasn't deep and the ground was soft, so Kate wasn't worried that Marcia would be hurt.

But . . .

This was awful.

What to do first? Yell at Angela for being a brat or rescue Marcia? Kate leaped off Tapestry. Already, Laura was on the ground, ready to take Tapestry's reins.

"Thanks," Kate said and bolted toward the trench. She peered down. "Are you okay?"

"Yes," Marcia said, looking up.

Orange mud stained her breeches, and her helmet had come off, but she didn't appear to be hurt. Instead, she squatted down and reached for something—a stone, maybe? Then, with a squeal, Marcia leaped backward as if she'd been stung.

"What is it?" Kate said.

She took a step closer to the edge and felt the ground crumble. Her foot slipped. Arms churning like a windmill, Kate tried to save herself, but down she went.

"Watch out," Angela yelled.

Her words echoed in Kate's brain as she slithered into the trench with Marcia, feet first and hands scrabbling for something to hold onto. It wasn't that dangerous, not like tumbling into a ravine or a cave, and not nearly as scary as what Kate had been through in Cornwall when she'd helped rescue Twiggy and Adam. Clumsily, Kate landed on her knees and immediately reached for Marcia.

"What did you find?"

"This," Marcia said. Sucking in her breath, she pointed at a small mound of something grayish-white poking from the side of the trench.

It looked like an old soccer ball. But was it, really? Kate peered closer. The mound had two oval holes and a longer, narrower one between them, like a—

Skull?

No, it couldn't be.

* * *

Angela tried to pretend it didn't matter. "It's probably a dead cow," she said, but Kate wouldn't let it go. She'd seen human skulls at the museum with her father.

And this was just like them.

Feeling shaky, she climbed out of the trench and hauled Marcia out behind her. Already, the other kids were squealing with excitement.

Nadine said, "I bet it's a murder."

"Or a kidnapping," said Maeve sounding awed.

Amber gave a short laugh. "A serial killer. Let's look for another one."

"Cereal?" said Eden. Her voice cracked. "Like cornflakes and Cap'n Crunch?"

"No, stupid," Gabrielle snapped. "Like when lots of—"

"Shut up," Laura said. "You're disgusting."

"Scaredy cat," taunted Maeve.

"That's enough," Kate said. She helped Marcia back into Daisy's saddle, then climbed into her own with legs that felt as wobbly as Jell-O.

"*Do* something," Angela said as if the whole fiasco were Kate's fault.

"Like what?"

"I dunno." Angela yanked out her cell phone, then slammed it back into her pocket. "Stupid thing."

No service, obviously. This was the deadest—Kate almost choked on the word—part of the mountain. Desperately, she looked around for help, but it was just her and Angela and eight little girls.

Why was there a skull in the trench?

Had the workmen left it there to freak them out?

Or was it a plastic toy from that tacky gift shop at the mall?

Questions bounced around Kate's brain like rocks in a tumbler. No way could they go on with the scavenger hunt. Not after this. They had to get back to the barn. Somebody needed to call the police. But suppose it really was just a plastic skull like the one at Sue and Brad's Halloween party last year. Maybe—

"Okay," Kate said, taking charge because it was obvious that Angela wasn't going to. "Angela, you go back to the barn, fast as you can, and tell—"

Angela shuddered. "I'm not going alone."

"Then stay here with the kids and—"

"No." Angela's face had gone pale.

"Okay, we'll all go," Kate said.

Really, it didn't matter if they got there fast or slow or somewhere in between. That horrible skull wasn't going anywhere. She turned toward the girls, still carrying on about ghouls and ghosts. Eden looked as if she were about to cry.

In a small voice, Charlotte said, "Is it real, Kate?"

"The skull?"

Charlotte gulped. "Yes."

"I think so," Kate said. "But we'll find out for sure, okay?"

"I don't *want* to know," the girl said. "It's too creepy."

Tossing her head, Tapestry danced sideways and shied at a tree stump she'd seen a million times before. Kate patted the mare's golden neck. "Easy, girl. It won't eat you."

They were all a bit freaked out, even the horses. Silly,

really. It was just an old skull and perfectly harmless, so what could it possibly do? Unless, of course, you believed in ghouls, ghosts, and zombies, which Kate didn't. Nevertheless, she'd feel better once they got back to the barn and dumped the problem into somebody else's lap.

* * *

Riding Pardner, Mr. Evans met them halfway home. He took one look at Kate and said, "What's wrong?"

It all spilled out.

The relief was enormous. Just telling a grown-up about what they'd found in the trench lifted a load off Kate's mind. Before heading off to investigate, Mr. Evans told the girls he would figure things out.

"Don't worry," he said. "Just enjoy that barbecue."

Kate sniffed. She could already smell it. Smoke from Aunt Bea's grill spiraled upward as they approached the barn. Holly ran up, holding hands with Adam.

"Did you get all the clues?"

"Kind of, but—"

Kids' voices drowned out her words. Nadine and Amber argued about how big the skull was, and Gabrielle said it was really awesome.

Maeve slid off her pony and pulled a face. "Gross," she said. "Totally gross."

Leading Tapestry into her stall, Kate filled Holly in.

"Bummer," Holly said.

"Why?"

"Because I missed it."

Kate was too drained to argue. Holly loved stuff like this. She read vampire books; she loved movies with ghouls and zombies—the creepier the better. But something about the skull they'd found wasn't creepy. It was sad. A real person had died, but they didn't have a proper grave marker. Nobody who loved them knew where they were.

12

For three days, nothing happened. Kate kept asking Aunt Bea if Mr. Evans had any answers about the skull, but all she did was purse her lips.

"He's working on it," she said. "Be patient."

But it wasn't easy. The kids were pestering Kate with questions and swapping silly jokes about zombies. Even Angela, who'd recovered her cool, now said it was no big deal. Kate didn't bother to remind her how freaked out she'd been.

Holly was still annoyed that she'd missed all the fun.

"It wasn't fun," Kate said.

"So, which team won?" Holly persisted.

"I think it was a draw."

That's what Aunt Bea said, even though Mrs. Dean objected. But Aunt Bea overruled her, and, miraculously,

Mrs. Dean had backed off. With the scavenger hunt now over, she was focusing her gaze on the final show, where the all-important parents would be in attendance. She'd ordered the Timber Ridge maintenance crew to spruce up the grandstand, paint the outside jumps, and make sure there was enough parking for all the fancy BMWs and Range Rovers.

"My dad drives a truck," Charlotte said.

"I'm sure they'll find room for it," Kate said.

So, the mysterious father was coming after all. Charlotte still hadn't said a word about him, despite Kate's questions and careful probing. It was as if he didn't quite exist; or if he did, Charlotte was doing her best to pretend otherwise.

* * *

On Wednesday, after having failed to line up any clinics, Mrs. Dean finally relented and allowed the camp kids to have a sleepover at Crescent Lake, in real tents. Except these weren't just any old tents. They had fringed awnings, wi-fi, and running water.

"Air conditioning?" Holly said.

Kate grimaced. "This isn't camping, it's—"

"Glamping," Angela said sounding smug.

"What's that?" Kate said.

They'd just been driven to the campsite in a fleet of Timber Ridge vans filled with picnic hampers, down quilts, first-aid supplies, and enough Evian water to float a submarine.

No ponies, though.

The kids had argued but Mrs. Dean held firm and Kate had to agree with her. Coping with eight excited little girls was tough enough; trying to corral eight even more excited ponies at the lake would put them over the top.

Holly whipped out her cell phone.

For once, there appeared to be service. "*Glamping*," she read out loud, "is a fusion of glamour and camping. When you're glamping, there's no tent to pitch, no sleeping bag to unroll, no fire to build."

"No fire?" Kate said. "What about s'mores and—?"

"All taken care of," Angela said waving toward the Timber Ridge foreman who was now unloading a portable fire pit from his shiny green truck. A helper stood by with fake logs and a garden hose at the ready.

Even that was carefully orchestrated. Along with the fire pit, Mrs. Dean had probably ordered designer skewers from Williams-Sonoma for the kids to roast gourmet marshmallows on. Their down quilts would match the décor, and whatever bugs managed to invade the tents' defensive screens would be color-coordinated. Kate suppressed a sigh. This whole scenario wasn't even remotely real, but she figured it was better than not camping at all.

"C'mon," Holly said as three little girls dashed past them waving masks and snorkels. "Let's go swimming."

"They won't see much in the lake," Kate said. She wasn't sure the lake even had any fish in it. It had a bazillion frogs, though. They'd probably keep everyone awake all night with their incessant chirping.

"That's not the point," Holly said. "And stop being a grump. Lighten up, okay?"

Kate shrugged. She was being a wet blanket, she knew that, but couldn't explain why. Maybe she was more worried about Mrs. Dean's dumb alpine slide than she realized. But that was kind of stupid. Worrying about it wouldn't solve the problem. Only action would. If only Dad were here. He'd know what to do.

"All right," Kate finally said.

But she dawdled in the counselors' tent, finding her bathing suit, and then climbing into it and rummaging around for her flip-flops. And by the time she was ready, Holly had disappeared with the kids. Shrieks echoed across the water as they cannonballed off the diving raft. Rapidly, Kate counted heads. Seven girls plus Holly and Kristina. Angela was lazing on a chaise beneath a weeping willow tree.

So which camper was missing?

Kate figured it out as she swam toward them. "Where's Charlotte?"

"In her tent," Kristina said, "last I saw."

Someone grabbed Kate from behind, and down she went, spluttering and laughing. Wildly, she lunged at a pair of legs and within seconds she was chasing Holly toward the raft. Little girls trailed in her wake like minnows following a dolphin.

Holly demonstrated a racing dive off the raft and showed Laura how to do the butterfly.

"I wanna learn," shouted Maeve.

"Me, too," Nadine yelled.

The others chimed in and Kate realized that these kids were a whole lot nicer in the water than on their ponies. Maybe just getting them away from the barn and the pressure of competition their parents put them through was enough to break the cycle. Well, whatever it was, Kate began to have fun and she forgot all about Charlotte Baker.

* * *

Looking around, Holly said, "Who's not here."

They were in the dining tent being served goat cheese and pineapple pizza by uniformed waiters from the Timber Ridge club house. A chunk of pineapple slid off Kate's fork and landed on the pristine white tablecloth. Hurriedly, she scooped it up. Across the table, the empty chair between Laura and Marcia stuck out like a first-grader's missing tooth.

"Charlotte," Kate said and felt immediately guilty. She hadn't even checked her team's tent after they'd gotten back from swimming. They'd all been too busy vying for the temporary showers. Hot water, no less. Kate had no idea where Mrs. Dean had conjured that from.

"So, where is she?" Holly said.

"Sulking," Nadine said.

"Why?"

"Because—"

"Never mind why," Kate said getting to her feet so fast that her chair tumbled backward. "What I want to know is where is she?"

But nobody knew.

Abandoning her pizza, Kate ran from tent to tent, opening flaps and calling Charlotte's name. This was her fault. She should've paid more attention. Over the past three days Charlotte had gotten quieter and quieter, but Kate had been so wrapped up in worrying about the skull and Mrs. Dean's dumb alpine slide, she'd failed to notice.

Holly caught up with her by the showers. Breathing hard, she handed Kate a flashlight. "Let's split up, and don't panic."

Easy for Holly to say.

Charlotte wasn't her responsibility. Kate had taken her on because she wanted to, just like she wanted to help Marcia Dean as well. In a way, she could see something of herself in both little girls. She'd once been in their shoes—awkward and shy, unable to make friends easily the way Holly and Jennifer did.

While Holly headed around the north side of the lake,

Kate combed the south side. Shadows danced across the ground; stumps and rocks took on ominous shapes in the gloom. Kate shuddered. If Charlotte were out here, she'd be scared stiff by now.

But why had she run off?

Kate switched her flashlight to full beam and maneuvered her way over rocks and through the brush. Last year she'd escaped out here by herself when it looked as if Tapestry might be taken from her. Maybe Charlotte was feeling the same way. Was she about to lose Elke?

No, that wouldn't happen. Charlotte's mother had bought Elke just a few months before. It had to be something else. Kate tried to remember what it was like to be ten years old, but she'd blanked out that part of her life. Her mother had died when Kate was nine—a year younger than Charlotte—and her father had retreated into his shell. After that, Kate had been pretty much on her own. She'd brought herself up and learned to look after her father as well.

"Old before her time," one of her aunts had said when she thought Kate wasn't listening.

Just then, she heard a noise.

It sounded like crying. That had to be Charlotte, but would she want Kate blundering into her private moments and making them even worse? The last time Kate had tried to help Holly with emotional stuff, she'd messed up so badly they'd ended up not speaking for a week.

"Go away," Charlotte said.

Kate stopped. "Okay."

There was a pause, the sound of Charlotte blowing her nose. "No, I—"

With one foot poised over the path, Kate hesitated. She didn't dare take another step in case snapping twigs or crumpling leaves might set Charlotte off. But she couldn't stand out here half the night on one leg like a stork.

Carefully, she inched closer. Charlotte was sitting on the very same rock that Kate had sat on last summer when she was convinced that Tapestry had been stolen and would be going back to her original owner. Remembering it all, Kate's heart thumped so loud and so hard, she felt sick.

"Are you all right?" she whispered.

A dumb thing to say, because of course Charlotte wasn't all right, but it was what everyone said when they didn't have the words for anything else. The moon peeked out from behind a cloud and briefly lit up Charlotte's face. A tear trickled down her cheek. She made no move to wipe it away.

"Yeah . . . no."

"Do you want company, or should I—?"

With a loud sniff, Charlotte waved toward another rock. Kate edged toward it and sat down. She leaned forward, elbows on her knees and her chin cupped with both hands. Moments passed. Charlotte didn't speak, and Kate knew that if she didn't try to start a conversation, they would be out here for hours, saying nothing.

She said, "If you want to talk, I'm ready to listen."

It took a few moments, but finally Charlotte let loose. "They're mean," she said, "and I hate them."

"Who?" Kate said.

It was pretty obvious who Charlotte meant, but Kate wanted to be sure. For all she knew, Charlotte could be talking about her parents or classmates from home or even her teachers.

"Gabrielle and Nadine," Charlotte said.

Kate opened her mouth to argue and shut it again. No point in trying to fake it. She hated herself for admitting it, but she didn't like those girls very much, either. "Tell me about it."

It all came tumbling out, how the other girls poked fun at Elke because she wasn't a sleek hunter pony and that Charlotte was a namby-pamby for not jumping. "They said I'll never win any ribbons."

"Ribbons aren't important," Kate said.

"Oh, yeah?" Charlotte said. "Tell that to Gabrielle. It's *all* she talks about. She's got so many ribbons that she doesn't have enough space in her bedroom to hang them all up."

"It's not about winning ribbons," Kate said, fumbling for the words her mother always used. "It's about feeling good about yourself and knowing that you tried your best."

Charlotte pulled a face. "But you've got lots of rib-bons."

"Who said?"

"Marcia."

And she was right. Kate had a ton of ribbons she'd won on Magician and Tapestry, and she'd have had even more if she hadn't trashed all the ribbons she'd won with Black Magic at her old barn in Connecticut.

Her heart skipped a beat.

It always did when she thought about Magic. He'd belonged to her former instructor and was slated to take Kate to the Young Riders' competition. But, the night before a big horse show, Magic had gotten out of his stall and into the feed room where he had gorged on grain. He'd colicked and died before anyone found him.

Kate had taken the blame.

She'd been the last person in the barn that night, and for three months she carried her guilt like a giant stone on her shoulders. It was only after she'd moved to Vermont that she found out another girl had been to the barn after her and that she was the one—not Kate—who'd neglected to bolt Magic's stall door properly.

"Marcia says Holly has lots of ribbons, too," Charlotte went on sounding almost defiant, as if she were now looking for an argument. "If ribbons aren't important, why are you winning them?"

Kate groaned.

She had no easy answer for this—at least, not in words that would connect with a ten-year-old. And even if Kate were able to find the right words, she'd probably make a terrible mess of saying them, just like she always made a mess of trying to explain her feelings to Holly or anyone else for that matter, including boys—especially boys.

Whoosh!

A burst of color—purple, green, and scarlet—erupted over the lake. Dazzling and twinkling, it fell back to earth in a silvery shower. Kate blinked.

Saved by fireworks?

"Let's go," she said reaching for Charlotte's hand. "We're missing all the fun."

13

WITH A SHOW OF DETERMINATION, Holly maneuvered another marshmallow onto her skewer and hoped it would stick this time. The last two had fallen into the fire, much to everyone's amusement.

"Don't you know how to do it?" Maeve asked.

Nadine cracked up. "Nah . . . she's too old."

"*Old*?" Holly said.

Whatever next? At any moment, these kids would have her in a coffin, along with zombies, vampires, and the walking dead.

And skulls.

The kids' camp fire stories kept coming back to that *thing*—whatever it was—that Kate and Marcia had found in Mrs. Dean's alpine slide. It sounded totally gross and Holly was beginning to think they'd made it all up. To distract herself, she glanced at Kate and wondered for the zillionth time if they'd ever find a way to get their own back at Angela for wrecking Mom's wedding dress.

If only someone else would do it.

Like last year, when Jennifer West invited Kate and Holly to Beaumont Park, her grandmother's equestrian center in England, and hadn't invited Angela as well. The horrified look on Angela's face when she discovered that she wasn't included was worth a dozen blue ribbons.

But how to pull it off this time?

Sue and Robin weren't around and Jennifer was still in England, which meant there was nobody else at the barn who cared enough to help out. Holly racked her brains but couldn't think of a single thing she and Kate could do to Angela that would embarrass her in front of an audience.

Holly sighed.

Maybe this time, they'd just have to give in and let Angela chalk up another win. She sat on the other side of the campfire, giggling with Kristina and hunched over her iPhone, geeking out over Luke Callahan's latest blue ribbon. Earlier, Mrs. Dean had handed out prize lists for the horse show, and now all the kids were reading them and having a meltdown.

"Ugh, I hate equitation," Amber said.

Maeve chimed in. "Me, too."

"What's *Family Pony*?" said Gabrielle.

It had been Holly's idea, based on a class at the show they'd attended in England. She explained that the ponies had to stand still while the kids dismounted and re-mounted, and then had to take them safely over low jumps without refusing or running out—oh, and not having a hissy fit over stuff like sack races and apple bobbing.

"What about our tack?" Eden said.

"And grooming?" Laura added.

Nadine snorted. "That's dumb stuff."

"Not," Holly said. "In Family Pony, you'll be judged on all of it."

Mrs. Dean had objected that this wasn't done at American shows until Holly pointed out that all the royal children entered the family pony classes in England. Holly had no idea if this were true, and she didn't care as long as it got Mrs. Dean's attention. More than likely the royals had never wielded a curry comb or a hoof pick in their lives, but Mrs. Dean didn't need to know that.

"Family ponies aren't temperamental show ponies," Holly went on. "They're good natured and bombproof."

"That lets out Sandcastle," Kate said.

Holly almost choked on a marshmallow.

The other events were typical horse show classes—hunter on the flat and over fences, show jumping, and trail. The kids could enter whatever they wanted. "The more the merrier" was Mrs. Dean's motto. She appeared determined to give out as many ribbons and Hershey kisses as possible.

Aunt Bea had agreed to judge the show. Mr. Evans would be the ring steward—as well as judge of the trail class—and he was at the barn right now, helping Aunt Bea take care of all the horses while the kids were having their campout.

"No favorites," Holly had warned.

Aunt Bea had bristled. "Of course not."

Seven years ago, she'd judged Holly's first walk-trot class and pinned her second from last. Filled with an eight-year-old's indignation, Holly had complained loudly to her mother and to Aunt Bea.

"I'm sorry," Aunt Bea had said, "but you weren't good enough. So get more practice and try harder next time."

Lesson learned.

"Aww," Marcia said as Holly's latest marshmallow fell off her skewer and burned to a crisp.

"Klutz," Kate said, laughing.

Egged on by the kids' giggles, Holly faked a ferocious glare. She complained this wasn't fair, that Kate's evenly tanned marshmallow was a fluke, never mind it slotted neatly between two layers of chocolate and the graham crackers that Mrs. Dean's catering staff had provided. Gritting her teeth, Holly took aim and speared another marshmallow from the bag. This time, she would make it work.

She really would.

And she almost did, except Angela stumbled past and bumped into her, knocking Holly's perfect marshmallow into the flames.

"Oh, *sorry*," Angela said not sounding sorry at all, just like she had over Mom's dress.

Holly's resolve hardened.

Somehow, she had to find a way to get even.

* * *

There was no sign of Aunt Bea or Mr. Evans when they got home at noon the next day. Kate glanced around the messy kitchen—an overturned chair, two half-empty cups of cold coffee, and toast crumbs all over the table. Vegetable soup spilled from a Dutch oven on the stove.

"Looks like they had a hurricane," Holly said.

"Or a tornado," Kate said, grabbing a bunch of paper towels to clean up the mess. What on earth had happened? Had Aunt Bea—?

Just then, Holly's cell phone rang. "Hello?" she said.

Kate watched Holly's face turn pale. "What's wrong?"

"It's Mr. Evans," Holly said covering the phone with her hand. "Aunt Bea's had an accident."

"How?" Kate said. "When?"

"Hush." Holly waved her off. "Yes, okay. Call me as soon as you know." She hung up and burst into tears.

Abandoning all thoughts of cleaning, Kate flipped the

chair upright and made Holly sit down. "Tell me what happened."

Haltingly, Holly explained that Aunt Bea had been making soup and picked up the heavy Dutch oven, but it slipped from her hands. She tried to save it from falling, and wrenched her shoulder instead. "She's torn two tendons," Holly said, wiping her eyes. "She's having surgery this afternoon."

Kate sat down hard on the other chair. "Surgery?"

"An operation," Holly said. "She'll be in the hospital for three days." She held up her cell phone. "I'm calling Mom."

"No."

"Why not?"

"She'll want to fly home," Kate said. "Right away."

Holly scowled. "But if we don't tell her, she'll ground us, like, *forever*."

"And if we *do* tell her and she flies home," Kate said, scowling back, "Aunt Bea will lock us in a closet and throw away the key." She thought for a minute. Liz and Dad would have a fit if the girls stayed by themselves for a couple of nights, so who could they ask for help?

As if reading her mind, Holly said, "What about Aunt Marion?"

Kate brightened. "Good idea," she said and was about to make the call when her cell phone jumped into action. It had been silent while they'd been at the campsite because cell service was pretty much non-existent on Timber Ridge Mountain. Caller ID said it was Mrs. Dean.

Oh, boy. Now what? More trouble?

After listening to yet more useless instructions from Mrs. Dean, Kate told her about Aunt Bea's accident.

"This is most inconvenient," Mrs. Dean said with an exasperated sigh. "I'll have to find another judge."

Easier said than done.

At this time of the year, all qualified judges in New England were booked solid. On the other hand, this wasn't an A-rated show, or even Z-rated. It was just a bunch of camp kids performing for their parents—and for Mrs. Dean, who'd probably bribe whatever judge she found to give the blue ribbons to kids with the richest parents.

At this point, Kate didn't care about judges. She just wanted the whole camp thing to be over so they could get back to normal, whatever that was. On Sunday her dad and Liz would be back from their honeymoon.

But not in time for the show.

*   *   *

The operation was successful. Aunt Bea's surgeon was able to repair the damage, and by the time Kate and Holly saw her on Friday morning, Aunt Bea was sitting up in her hospital bed and insisting she felt good enough to come home.

Mr. Evans shook his head. "Not till your doctor says it's okay to leave."

"But," Aunt Bea protested, "the show—"

"—will go on without you," he said.

"Mrs. Dean's finding another judge," Kate said.

Wincing slightly, Aunt Bea leaned back into her pillow. "Maybe she'll hire George Morris."

"Or Sam Callahan," said Holly.

They all laughed, even Mr. Evans, who probably didn't recognize the famous names. They were hunter-jumper people, not Western riders like him.

Kate said, "How about Lockie Malone?"

He'd given a dressage clinic at Timber Ridge in January, but Kate had just messed up her knee—skiing with Brad—and had been unable to ride. She'd crossed paths with Lockie again at the Festival of Horses, where he'd admired Tapestry and had then told Holly that if she ever wanted to sell Magician to let him know.

Holly sighed. "He's totally dishy."

* * *

Back at the barn, things were bordering on chaos. Angela and Kristina had lost control, and half the kids were running wild. Rakes and pitchforks littered the aisle, muck buckets overflowed, and nobody was cleaning tack, which is what Kate had told them to do while she and Holly were at the hospital. Holding hands, Nadine and Amber bopped about to *One Direction*'s latest hit, which blared from the barn's scratchy old radio.

Kate snapped it off. "Listen up, you guys."

She wanted to rant and rave at them, but it wouldn't do any good. These were privileged kids with parents who'd slam her if she laid into them for slacking off. A quick glance at Holly told Kate that her new sister felt the same way.

Cool it, Holly mouthed.

It only took a few minutes to calm everyone down, but that was because Laura and Marcia, looking embarrassed for having goofed off, pitched in to help organize things. They ushered Maeve, Amber, and Nadine into the tack room and told Gabrielle and Eden to get busy mucking stalls.

"What shall I do?" said Charlotte.

"Give your pony a bath," Kate said. "She's got grass stains on her knees." She led Elke into the wash stall, handed Charlotte a bucket and a bottle of shampoo, and told her to get busy.

Charlotte saluted. "Yes, ma'am!"

Outside, the Timber Ridge crew was putting the finishing touches to Mrs. Dean's last-minute improvements. Jumps sparkled with fresh paint, plump seat cushions dotted the small grandstand, and the barn's parking lot had been raked smooth like a grand prix arena. A gate that opened and closed had been built for the trail class, along with a sturdy bridge for the bravest ponies to walk over. Red and white petunias tumbled from window boxes. Elke would have a grand time with those.

14

SHOW DAY DAWNED BRIGHT AND CLEAR. Kate hauled herself out of bed and snagged the bathroom before Holly even opened her eyes. By this time tomorrow, camp would be almost over and most of the kids would be going home with their ponies. Apart from Marcia and Laura, the only one Kate would miss was Charlotte Baker.

Whoever had advised her mother to buy the Norwegian Fjord had been absolutely right. That pony was perfect for Charlotte—sturdy and reliable and totally bombproof. If they didn't win family pony—and the trail class—Kate would shred the judge.

Never mind who it was.

And never mind what she'd said about winning. At this point in her life, Charlotte needed a confidence boost, and a few ribbons would do it nicely—whether to vindicate her mother for buying Elke or to impress her father, who sounded difficult, if not impossible, to please.

Maybe he wouldn't show up.

That would be best. Then Charlotte could relax and not worry about him criticizing her in front of all her friends, like he'd apparently done at the last show she'd competed in. Gently, Kate had pressed Charlotte for details, but the little girl had clammed up. Kate dragged on her jeans and a pair of paddock boots. Holly began to stir.

"What time is it?" she mumbled from beneath a tangle of sheets.

"Six thirty."

"Ugh!"

"I'll feed," Kate said.

Holly yawned. "Thanks."

Kate felt a rush of affection for her brand-new stepsister, then realized this was the first time she'd even thought of Holly as a *stepsister*. It smacked of Cinderella and the uglies—kind of like Marcia and Angela—and look how that had worked out.

No, Kate decided. *Stepsister* was off limits.

From now on, she and Holly were *real* sisters no matter what anyone else—including Angela and Mrs. Dean—thought of them.

* * *

Someone had beaten Kate to the barn. The horses were already munching hay and looking over their stall doors, whickering anxiously for grain.

"Who's there?" Kate called.

From the feed room, Marcia said, "Me and Laura."

"And me," Charlotte said.

She emerged with an armload of buckets, and Kate hoped they were all correctly measured. It wasn't easy to feed this crowd, given the different minerals and supplements that each horse required.

"Let me see," Kate said.

Charlotte held out her buckets. "We followed instructions."

They were written on a white board in the feed room, and Kate relaxed when she saw that the girls had got it right, including the splash of molasses that Nadine's pony, Hijack, needed to get him to eat.

"Well done."

With a shy grin, Charlotte took off, tipping feed into each horse's bucket. Marcia walked behind with the hose and topped up their water while Laura dragged out a pitchfork and began cleaning stalls.

For a moment, Kate felt superfluous.

This was the new generation of Timber Ridge Riders. Was she this competent at their age? She couldn't remember. The barn door opened and Holly staggered inside, still yawning and wearing ripped jeans.

"What have I missed?"

"A seismic shift," Kate said.

"Plate tectonics?"

"Not quite, but close."

"Oh, good," Holly said. "Is there any coffee?"

Half an hour later, two guys from Mrs. Dean's maintenance crew showed up to help. They swamped out the remaining stalls, emptied muck buckets, raked the aisle, and climbed ladders to sweep cobwebs off the rafters.

"Pity they didn't do this sooner," Kate said as the men trundled off.

"PR," Holly muttered.

"What's that?"

"Public relations. Mrs. Dean wants to impress the parents." Holly rolled her eyes and struck a pose. "We have a *show* barn here," she said in Mrs. Dean's exaggerated drawl. "Our riders win prizes at all the *best* events, you know."

Kate pretended to gag.

Behind them, she heard Marcia and Laura giggling.

* * *

At noon, everyone was invited to a gourmet brunch at the Timber Ridge club house. Holly and Adam, who'd showed up earlier, decided to go. Kate stayed behind. She wasn't in the mood to make small talk with Mrs. Dean's wealthy clients.

Marcia stayed behind, too.

She groomed Tapestry and cleaned her tack, even though she'd cleaned it thoroughly the night before. The show would begin at two o'clock, and, as Marcia told Kate, she was determined to be ready.

Slowly, the grandstand filled up. Important guests sat beneath a striped awning, sipping tall drinks and nibbling on canapés served by waiters wearing green polo shirts with the Timber Ridge logo. Small dogs yapped and strained at their leashes; expensive cars purred into the parking lot. A vendor with a colorful cart beneath a yellow umbrella dispensed large bags of gourmet popcorn. Another handed out soft drinks for the kids.

Kate kept her eye out for the new judge but didn't recognize anyone. Was it that guy with the tweed cap that all English trainers wore? For a horrible, heart-stopping moment, Kate thought it might be Vincent King. It would be just like Mrs. Dean to hire the evil trainer who'd been kicked out of Timber Ridge last summer.

But no. It was somebody else.

With a sigh of relief, Kate glanced at the woman beside him. Wearing a floppy straw hat, platform sandals, and oversized sunglasses, she didn't look like much of a horsewoman. But they were both chatting with Mrs. Dean.

"Who's that?" Kate said.

Holly shrugged. "Dunno."

Mrs. Dean looked about ready to make an announcement when Mr. Evans showed up with Aunt Bea in a wheelchair, her right arm supported by a complicated looking sling. With them was a man Kate had never seen before. He was tall and thin with a sharp nose and piercing brown eyes. Looking directly at Kate, he gave a small nod as if he knew her.

"Why a wheelchair?" Kate asked Holly.

She rolled her eyes. "My aunt tripped, right before she left the hospital, and sprained her ankle."

"Typical," Kate said, grinning.

"Ladies and gentlemen," Mrs. Dean squawked through the microphone. Her voice startled several ponies. "Thank you for coming, and please welcome our judges, Sam Callahan and Jocelyn Fraser, who've kindly donated their time to help us out."

Kate did a double-take.

Sam Callahan?

"Oh, my god," she gasped.

It was like watching royalty or celebrities on TV. Transfixed, Kate couldn't move a muscle as both judges shook hands with Mrs. Dean and then took up their stations in the center of the ring. How had Angela's mother managed to snag Sam Callahan? Jocelyn Fraser was a no-brainer. She'd already blown them off once and was probably doing this to make up for it.

But Sam Callahan?

He was Kate's hero—the guy who wrote articles for

Chronicle of the Horse and coached the U.S. show-jumping team. And he was right here, standing less than fifty feet away.

Oh, wow. Double wow.

* * *

By two o'clock the small grandstand was almost full, and Kate wondered which of the parents belonged to Charlotte. She scanned the crowd. Charlotte said her mom was coming alone, but everyone here seemed to be part of a large family group. On the bottom row, a dark haired woman sat by herself, reading a magazine and ignoring everyone else.

Maybe that was Mrs. Baker.

There was no sign of a man on his own or with a boy who could be Charlotte's brother. Maybe Mr. Baker hadn't shown up yet, or perhaps he'd decided not to come.

Cheerfully, Mrs. Dean announced class number one, hunter over fences. Nadine and Hijack won it handily, with Amber and Maeve taking second and third. All the kids got ribbons and a small bag of Hershey kisses, except for Charlotte, who hadn't entered this class.

Next up was hunter on the flat, and Amber snagged first place. Laura was fourth with Eden and Marcia tied for fifth. Again, everyone got kisses and a ribbon, and again, Charlotte hadn't entered.

"I didn't feel like it," she said, shrugging.

"How about equitation, then?" Kate said. Now that Charlotte had learned to relax, she was a reasonably competent rider, better than half the others.

"No."

"If you ride in the class, it'll get Elke warmed up for family pony and trail," Kate said. This wasn't really necessary. Elke never needed warming up. She was always the same—steady and predictable, no matter if she'd been cooped up in a stall for three days or frolicking outside in the paddock.

"Oh, all right." With a sigh, Charlotte gathered up her reins and trotted into the ring. The sun created dapples on Elke's blond rump; her bristly mane stuck up like a striped toothbrush. How could anyone *not* love this charming pony?

The others were already walking along the rail. After a complete circuit, Sam Callahan called for a trot, then back to a walk, and into a canter. Kate held her breath. This was the moment when Tapestry often let off a small buck. High spirits? Exuberance? Something to make her rider pay attention?

But Marcia was ready.

She kept Tapestry's head up and urged her forward, transitioning into a collected canter. Nose tucked, around the arena she went, looking like a dressage horse. Other ponies passed on the inside, but Tapestry didn't falter.

After much consultation, the judges pinned Laura and

Soupçon first, with Marcia and Tapestry in second place. As Jocelyn Fraser handed Marcia the red ribbon, Kate couldn't stop smiling. Now, maybe Mrs. Dean would wake up and realize that her former stepdaughter was a dynamite little horsewoman.

The rest of the class got pinned, and Kate's smile faded when she saw that Charlotte had wound up in last place. She didn't deserve that. Her equitation was far better than Gabrielle's, who'd placed third, despite the fact that Sandcastle had tried to take a bite out of Jocelyn Fraser's straw hat.

Charlotte's face was pinched, and she looked close to tears as she left the ring. She shot a look at Kate that said, *See, I told you I didn't want to do it.* Kate wanted to comfort her but didn't have a chance because Marcia and Laura immediately claimed her attention.

"Wasn't Tapestry *fabulous*?" Marcia exclaimed. Leaning forward, she flung her arms around the mare's neck and hugged her so hard she almost fell off.

"Yes," cried Laura hugging her own pony as well. "But Soupy was better."

Kate left them teasing one another and went to find Charlotte, but she'd disappeared. On her way to the barn she passed Angela, clinging onto the arm of a really cute guy. A lock of dark hair fell across his forehead as he glanced at Kate.

She'd seen him before, but where?

Angela's old boyfriend, Channing Alexander, was blond and wouldn't be caught dead anywhere near a horse barn. This guy was obviously new.

"Hi," he said as Kate raced past.

Why was his face so familiar? No time to think about it now. Elke was in her stall, still tacked up, but there was no sign of her rider. The show was taking a short break. Classes would resume in twenty minutes.

After checking the tack room and Liz's office, Kate found Charlotte in the feed room perched on a bale of hay, picking at her fingernails. A drop of blood oozed from her thumb, and Kate wanted desperately to mop it up and cover it with a Band-Aid—whatever it took to make Charlotte feel better—to let her know that somebody cared.

"Hey, what's wrong?" she said.

"Nothing."

"Is your mom here?"

Charlotte shrugged. "Yeah, I guess."

So why hadn't she gone to meet her? The other kids had swarmed the grandstand, having extravagant reunions with their parents as if they'd been away for two years rather than two weeks. As far as Kate knew, Charlotte hadn't been anywhere near the grandstand. She'd either been in the barn or out by the ring ever since she'd gotten back from Mrs. Dean's brunch.

"Didn't you see her at the club?"

"She wasn't there." Another shrug, more nail picking.

Then Charlotte dropped her hand and grabbed her braid instead. She stuck the tip in her mouth. "Mom can never get anywhere on time."

"What about your dad? Is he here?"

No answer. Just an awkward silence. From the aisle, Kate heard Holly warning the kids that classes were about to start up again. "Hustle," she yelled. "And don't forget to tighten your girths."

"Do you want to quit?" Kate said, looking at Charlotte and wishing she could say something—*anything*—that would help. A tear trickled down the girl's pale cheek.

She sniffed. "No."

"Then let's get going." Kate held out her hand. She didn't know what else to do. Coping with Charlotte and whatever issues she had with her parents was way above Kate's ability. She had no skills for this. Someone like Aunt Bea, or even Holly, would be able to figure the little girl out, but Kate was stumped.

15

An elaborate display of ribbons and prizes sat on a table beneath a green umbrella, presided over by a stern-faced woman who looked as if she'd slap anyone's hand if they so much as touched a chocolate kiss.

"Mrs. Dean's ugly twin sister?" Holly said.

Kate grimaced. The woman bore a striking resemblance to Angela's mother. "How is she scoring this?"

"Dunno," Holly said. "Does it matter?"

"Not really," Kate said.

But it did. She just didn't want to admit, even to Holly, how much she wanted Charlotte and Marcia to win ribbons. And, if she were brutally honest with herself, she wanted one of them to win the red, yellow, and blue championship ribbon and the giant Hershey kiss. Wrapped in shiny gold foil, it sat atop a silver cake stand like a real trophy.

During the break, the ring crew had set up jumps— nothing over two and a half feet—and they all had flower boxes, brightly painted poles, and white wings, except for the coop, which had gaudy wooden chickens the size of Godzilla standing to attention on each side.

Tapestry would probably freak out.

She hated coops and was highly suspicious of chickens. When Kate had first seen her, Tapestry was trapped inside a field strewn with junk cars, a dilapidated coop, and plastic bags spewing garbage. Half a dozen evil looking chickens had wandered around, pecking at anything that moved, especially Tapestry's feet.

"Watch out for the coop," Kate warned Marcia as she waited her turn to jump. "Tapestry will try to run out. Just keep your legs on her and—"

Marcia grinned. "She'll be okay."

"How do you know?"

"Because I already showed her the chickens," Marcia said, grinning even wider. "They were hidden behind the barn, and I knew Tapestry was scared, so we kind of made friends with them."

"How?"

"I bribed her with carrots," Marcia said, and Kate burst out laughing because that was exactly what she had done the year before when faced with the scary chicken coop while practicing for a show. She patted Marcia's highly polished boot.

"Good luck," she said as the bell rang.

Laura and Nadine had already gone clear. Eden had eight faults, Amber's pony racked up two refusals, and Sandcastle had gotten Gabrielle eliminated by bucking her off. Kate held her breath. Watching Marcia jumping Tapestry was a whole lot harder than doing it herself.

Over the blue crossrails they went, then the tiny yellow hogsback. The in-and-out was no problem, followed by an awkward leap over the green-and-white double oxer. Tapestry's hind foot caught a rail, and the crowd went, "Ahh." The rail rocked in its cups but didn't fall. Next came the red wall and Tapestry cleared it with inches to spare. One more to go—the dreaded coop. Its giant chickens glowed neon orange in the mid-afternoon sun.

"Don't stop, *please*," Kate muttered.

But Tapestry slowed. She dodged left, then right, and dirt flew from her hooves as she slid to a standstill. From the corner of her eye, Kate saw Angela and that boy sitting on the grandstand's top row. Angela was leaning against him, talking a mile a minute, but the boy was watching Tapestry, hand raised in a fist, almost as if he were willing her to get over that miserable coop.

Firmly, Marcia turned Kate's mare in a circle and headed for the jump again. One stride, two, and—

Another stop?

Kate closed her eyes and crossed her fingers. She would've crossed her toes as well if they hadn't been squashed inside her paddock boots. The crowd went, "Ahh," again and Kate opened one eye, expecting to see a second refusal. But Tapestry and Marcia were safely on the other side of the coop, cantering through the finish line.

"She made it," Holly said, grabbing Kate's arm. "Four faults. They're in third place."

"Whoopee!" Kate punched the air with her fist and then glanced at Angela's new beau. Slowly, he raised his hand and waved, as if saluting her.

Last to go was Maeve.

One jump after another fell. It was like watching a demolition derby. Maeve's pony had done well in the hunter over fences class, but show jumping was obviously not his thing. They racked up so many faults that Kate lost count.

After a jump-off, Nadine took first, with Laura in second place. Marcia was third and Eden a surprising fourth. Kate tried to figure out the overall standings but without knowing Mrs. Dean's scoring method, she was lost. No doubt it would be rigged in favor of the families Angela's mother most wanted to attract to Timber Ridge.

But Holly told her not to worry. Aunt Bea had set up the points system and said that Mrs. Dean wasn't smart enough to change it. "Math isn't her strongest skill," Holly said.

* * *

In preparation for Family Pony, the ring crew cleared the jumps to one side, leaving just the crossrail in place. It was low enough for Elke to step over.

"Are you okay with it?" Kate asked Charlotte.

Gloomily, she nodded. "I think so."

Then Mrs. Dean announced that Jocelyn Fraser would be judging the class by herself because Mr. Callahan had another engagement. There was a round of polite applause as the famous trainer doffed his cap and left the ring.

Visibly, Charlotte brightened. She sat up straighter, as if a sack of grain had been lifted from her shoulders; she began to smile. Even her pony seemed happier. But Kate was totally bummed out. She'd wanted to talk to Mr. Callahan, if only to let him know how much she loved his column in the *Chronicle*.

She sighed. "Oh, no."

"Cheer up," Holly said. "At least Miss Picture Perfect won't be judging trail as well."

Just then, Marcia's father strode up. He reached for Kate's hand and shook it so hard her eyeballs rattled. "I can't thank you enough," he said. "You've made my daughter very happy."

"Marcia's a great kid," Kate said.

"And she's had a great camp," Mr. Dean said. "I'm wondering if—" He hesitated. "I don't know quite how to put this, but would you be interested in selling Tapestry to us?"

Sell Tapestry?

"I had a word with Mr. Callahan," Henry Dean went on before Kate had a chance to speak. "He says your mare is worth ten thousand dollars. I'm prepared to pay double."

Kate gasped. Her knees buckled, and if it weren't for Holly holding her up, she'd have landed in a messy heap on the ground. A dozen thoughts raced through her mind.

Mr. Dean was enormously rich. Twenty thousand dollars was chump change to him. Last fall he'd wanted to reward Kate and Holly for rescuing Marcia from the Halloween blizzard, and when they refused, he'd invested a bundle of money in Dad's new business instead. Without Mr. Dean's generosity, Dad would never have been able to buy the butterfly museum.

But no. A bazillion times no.

She would never sell Tapestry, even if Mr. Dean offered her a million dollars. "I'm sorry," she blurted. "But I can't."

"Then, how about a lease?" he said. "Think about it, please. Tapestry would stay here because I'm buying another house at Timber Ridge. Marcia and I will be here every weekend and all through the summer."

Desperately, Kate looked at Holly.

Help, she mouthed.

* * *

Holly's heart did a triple somersault. This was wonderful and awful and scary, all at the same time. She knew how much Kate wanted to move forward with her riding and that Tapestry—as fabulous as she was—couldn't take her there.

While Kate stared at Mr. Dean, his former wife called for Family Pony to enter the ring. In talking about this class with her friends in England, Holly had learned that a lot of judges pinned the show ponies anyway, which was grossly unfair.

But Miss Picture Perfect surprised her—especially after she ordered the kids to dismount and get back on again. To everyone's delight, Marcia made Tapestry lie down, then climbed on board and told the mare to get up. As Tapestry lurched to her feet with Marcia safely in the saddle, people cheered and whistled; Angela's new boyfriend stood up and yelled, "Way to go."

Tapestry won the class.

Holly squealed and thumped Kate on the back as Marcia rode her victory lap, the coveted blue ribbon fluttering from Tapestry's bridle. Behind them, in second place, came Charlotte. Eden was third and Laura fourth.

"We swept it," Holly said.

Kate looked at her. "We did?"

"Our camp kids—one, two, three, and four."

Adam tried to give Kate a high five. Her hand trembled, and she looked as if she didn't quite know what to do with it. Henry Dean had rushed off to congratulate his daughter, but Kate was clearly in a serious swivet over his offer.

"We'll figure it out," Holly said, trying to reassure her. But the truth was, she had no clue what to do. When Lockie Malone wanted to know if Magician was for sale, Holly had been knocked into a tailspin. She'd been just as shell-shocked as Kate was now.

But this was how it worked.

When riders with Olympic-sized ambitions outgrew their horses, they sold them—or retired them—and bought better horses or found well-heeled sponsors who'd buy horses for them. They couldn't afford to get sentimental over horses that weren't capable of reaching the next level, no matter how much they loved them.

Was this what Kate wanted?

Holly didn't. She would never sell Magician, not ever, no matter what anyone offered. She would cut off her right arm before letting anyone take Magician away from her.

But a lease for Tapestry?

All things considered, this might be the best of both worlds. If Marcia's dad leased Tapestry, she'd still be at the barn and Kate would get to ride her, plus she'd have another, more talented horse, to bring along.

Yeah, right.

A horse like the one Kate wanted would cost at least twenty thousand dollars. Probably more. She'd only be able to afford it if she actually sold Tapestry to the Deans, and Holly just couldn't see that happening.

At least, not right now.

* * *

An excited murmur rose from the audience as Mr. Evans directed the ring crew to set up the trail class. There was the usual gate to open, a bridge to walk over, and window boxes filled with flowers for the horses to back between. But what caused the biggest stir was a curtain of swimming-pool noodles hanging like oversized spaghetti from a board suspended between two uprights.

"Yikes," Holly said. "That'll freak everyone out."

And it did, except for Elke who just sauntered through the candy-colored noodles, batting them with her head as if she were merely swatting flies.

She won the class, hands down.

Charlotte cantered her victory lap with an ear-splitting grin, followed by Eden and Laura. By this time, Kate had lost track of who had won the most points, but that didn't matter. Charlotte had the blue.

As all the kids gathered around Kate and Holly, Angela and the dark-haired boy strolled past, arm in arm. With his free hand he reached for Elke's reins. "Great job," he said.

Angela scoffed. "That pony's a cart horse. It doesn't belong in a show barn."

"Really?" he said scratching Elke's poll. He glanced at Kate, and she knew she'd seen him before. But where? Eyes narrowed, he looked down at Angela still clinging to his arm like a cheap dress. "Why not?"

"Because I think she's plug ugly, and—"

"It doesn't matter what *you* think," he said. "It's all about what my sister thinks. Right Charlotte?"

She grinned. "Thanks, Luke."

"But—" Angela said.

He interrupted. "I helped our mother choose this pony for my sister, okay?" His voice held a hint of steel.

Immediately, Angela shriveled into herself. She turned several shades of red as the boy gently, but firmly, pushed her away. Maeve and Nadine giggled.

Amber said, "I guess he doesn't like her any more."

"Yeah," said Gabrielle. "She's a loser."

Head down, Angela stumbled off by herself. For a moment, Kate felt almost sorry for her, then remembered what Angela had done to Liz's wedding dress and how she'd been rude to Mr. Evans and all the other times she'd hurt people.

No, this was perfect, just perfect.

Public humiliation in front of the rich little camp kids. Kate felt Holly nudging her. They'd gotten their own back on Angela without lifting a finger.

The boy shrugged. "Oh, well."

Kate shot another look at him. He was cute, in an ordinary sort of way—dark brown hair, greenish-brown eyes, and a nose that wasn't too big or too small. But there was something about him that made you look twice. His smile, maybe? Whatever it was, Kate couldn't put her finger on it and she couldn't stop looking at him.

Charlotte had called him Luke.

Luke?

All of a sudden, it smacked her between the eyes. Of course, she'd seen him before, like all over the place—the *Chronicle*'s front cover, Dover Saddlery's Facebook page, and the YouTube videos that Angela had obsessed over.

This was Lucas Callahan, the boy wonder of show jumping, and he was Charlotte Baker's brother. He was also Sam Callahan's son, and—

Holy moly.

Kate felt her legs go weak all over again.

16

THE LOUDSPEAKERS CRACKLED. Everyone turned toward Mrs. Dean who was now standing on her podium and looking none too pleased.

"What's up with her?" Holly said.

Kate shrugged. She was still in a turmoil over Mr. Dean's offer and meeting Luke Callahan. After giving Kate a thumbs-up for teaching Tapestry to lie down, Luke had wandered off with Charlotte and Elke, arm draped casually across the Fjord's ample rump and telling his sister how proud he was of her. Faintly, Kate heard him say, "Don't worry about Dad. He'll come around."

So, what did that mean?

In the past few days, Charlotte had left ambiguous hints about her dad's feelings toward Elke. Did he disapprove of her? If so, why? The Fjord was perfect for Charlotte—unless her father hated Elke because his ex-wife had bought her. Or was it something else, like the fact that Charlotte didn't use his last name? Kate sighed. Grown-ups could be so complicated.

With a face like thunder, Mrs. Dean announced the reserve champion. "Our runner-up"—she almost choked on the words—"is Marcia Dean, riding Tapestry owned by Kate McTavish."

"McGregor," someone shouted.

Holly jumped up and down. "Yippee!"

"Wowee!" Kate yelled.

She didn't even care that Mrs. Dean had gotten her name wrong. Others joined in the noisy celebration, including Aunt Bea, who'd been wheeled over from the grandstand by Mr. Evans. They were all cheering so loudly that Kate almost missed hearing about the grand champion.

"Laura Gardner with Soupçon," announced Mrs. Dean, who didn't sound much happier about this, either.

"Sour puss," Holly said.

Holding hands and squealing, Marcia and Laura ran up to get their ribbons and prizes. Parents took photos and even the non-winners cheered. Mrs. Dean's scowl deepened as she presented both girls with their giant Hershey kisses.

"I want some of that," Holly yelled.

"Me, too," echoed Kate.

Just then, Mr. Evans caught her attention and asked for a minute of her time—in private.

Kate shrugged. "Sure."

She followed him to the barn's side door, far away from the in-gate. With him was the tall man Kate had seen earlier. Mr. Evans introduced him as David Wickett. For a moment, the name didn't register. Then Kate remembered. This was Mr. Evans's old college roommate who worked for the governor.

"Hi," she said.

The man nodded but didn't speak. His face was grave, like he'd just received bad news, or maybe he wasn't a person who smiled easily.

"It's about that skull you found," Mr. Evans said.

In all the trauma and excitement, Kate had forgotten about Mrs. Dean's alpine slide. She forced herself to focus. This was important. Super important. A couple of ponies trotted by. Kate stood back to let them pass.

"What about it?" she said. At this point, the whole thing seemed like a dream. So much had happened since then that Kate had begun to wonder if she'd imagined it all.

Mr. Evans nodded at his friend. "David, I'll let you take over."

The Abenaki chief's voice was deep and cultured—he sounded faintly British—and it was obvious he knew exactly what he was talking about. Kate listened, enthralled and horrified, and the minute he was finished, she thanked him and ran off to find Holly.

Mr. Evans and Mr. Wickett were going to speak to Mrs. Dean, and while Kate got the feeling they didn't want her there, she absolutely could not miss it. Neither could her sister.

"What's wrong?" Holly said when Kate hauled her away from the kids who were helping Laura and Marcia demolish their Hershey kisses. Holly had a smear of chocolate across her chin.

"Come with me and don't argue," Kate said.

"Why?"

There wasn't time to explain. Holly would find out when they hid behind the grandstand, close enough to watch David Wickett send Mrs. Dean's plans for Timber Ridge into free fall.

* * *

Holly knew better than to argue with her sister. When Kate got like this—all steely eyed and determined—you just had to follow along and hope she didn't lead you down a rabbit hole.

Like Marines on maneuvers, they crept around the back of the barn, ducking behind farm equipment and the manure pile, en route to the grandstand. Mrs. Dean was at her podium, fussing with papers—probably the scoring sheets that she was so unhappy about—and still looking grim. In front of her stood Mr. Evans and another man.

"Who's that?" Holly said.

"David Wickett," Kate said. "He's the Abenaki chief Mr. Evans went to college with."

"Oh, right," Holly said.

Crouching beside Kate, she peered through the bleachers. They had a pretty good view. Nobody else was around except for a couple of parents who were too busy talking to pay attention to Mrs. Dean.

"What's all this about?" Mrs. Dean's voice boomed across the show grounds. Several heads turned, and something snapped loudly as Angela's mother turned off her microphone.

"Whoops," Holly said.

Kate rounded on her. "Hush."

Even without the microphone, Holly could hear quite clearly what was going on as Mr. Evans's friend told Mrs. Dean that she couldn't build her alpine slide on that particular slope because it was a sacred Indian burial ground.

Mrs. Dean bristled. "I don't care about that."

"But Vermont does," said David Wickett.

They went back and forth, arguing about state laws and stuff that Holly didn't understand, but in the end, Mrs. Dean appeared to back down. Her shoulders sagged, her face lost its fire, and she almost fell off the podium.

"We've won," Kate said.

"What do you mean?" Holly said, still confused

"No alpine slide."

"Really?"

"Yes, really," Kate said. "Mrs. Dean's bulldozers dug up an Indian burial ground. But they're protected by Vermont law, so—"

"—no more theme park?"

Kate shook her head. "Not for now, anyway."

This was good enough for Holly, and she was still fist bumping with Kate when her mother and Kate's dad arrived home from their honeymoon, a day sooner than expected. Mom glowed with happiness, like she could step onto a cloud if one drifted down low enough to pick her up.

Ben's beard tickled Holly's cheek as he swept her into a hug and swung her around until she was almost dizzy. Then Mom said, "So, did we miss anything?"

"No, not much," Kate said.

Holly rolled her eyes and gave her brand-new sister a high five. After a second or two, they both laughed so hard that Holly thought for sure her sides would burst wide open.

Sign up for our mailing list and be among the first to know when the next Timber Ridge Riders book will be out. Send your email address to:

timberridgeriders@gmail.com

For more information about the series, visit: www.timberridgeriders.com

or check out our Facebook page: www.facebook.com/TimberRidgeRiders

Note: all email addresses are kept strictly confidential.

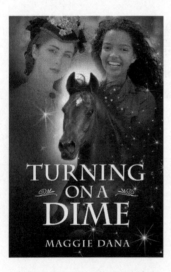

Two girls, two centuries apart, and the horse that brings them together

TURNING ON A DIME

This exciting time-travel adventure (with horses, of course) from the author of TIMBER RIDGE RIDERS is available in print and ebook from your favorite book store.

for information: www.maggiedana.com

About the Author

MAGGIE DANA'S FIRST RIDING LESSON, at the age of five, was less than wonderful. She hated it so much, she didn't try again for another three years. But all it took was the right horse and the right instructor and she was hooked.

After that, Maggie begged for her own pony and was lucky enough to get one. Smoky was a black New Forest pony who loved to eat vanilla pudding and drink tea, and he became her constant companion. Maggie even rode him to school one day and tethered him to the bicycle rack . . . but not for long because all the other kids wanted pony rides, much to their teachers' dismay.

Maggie and Smoky competed in Pony Club trials and won several ribbons. But mostly, they had fun—trail riding and hanging out with other horse-crazy girls. At horse camp, Maggie and her teammates spent one night sleeping in the barn, except they didn't get much sleep because the horses snored. The next morning, everyone was tired and cranky, especially when told to jump without stirrups.

Born and raised in England, Maggie now makes her home on the Connecticut shoreline. When not mucking stalls or grooming shaggy ponies, Maggie enjoys spending time with her family and writing the next book in her TIMBER RIDGE RIDERS series.

15777500R00107

Printed in Great Britain
by Amazon